Come to Me

Come to Me

Stories

Amy Bloom

Aaron Asher Books
HarperCollins*Publishers*

The following stories appeared in slightly different form in these publications: "Love Is Not a Pie" in *Room of One's Own* (1990), *Image* (Ireland, 1991), and *Best American Short Stories*, 1991; "Sleepwalking" in *River City* (Fall 1991); "The Sight of You" in *Story* (Summer 1992); "Silver Water" in *Story* (Autumn 1991) and *Best American Short Stories, 1992*; "Semper Fidelis" in *Antaeus* (April 1993); "When the Year Grows Old" in *Story* (Winter 1992).

HarperCollins books may be purchased for educational, business, or sales promotional use. For information, please write: Special Markets Department, Harper-Collins Publishers, Inc., 10 East 53rd Street, New York, NY 10022.

FIRST EDITION

Designed by C. Linda Dingler

Library of Congress Cataloging-in-Publication Data
Bloom, Amy, 1953–
  Come to me : short stories / Amy Bloom.
    p. cm.
  ISBN 0-06-018236-9
  I. Title.
PS3552.L6378C65 1993
813'.54—dc20   92-54725

93 94 95 96 97 ❖/RRD 10 9 8 7 6

For Donald,
most, best, and always

Contents

Come to Me

Love Is Not a Pie

In the middle of the eulogy at my mother's boring and heart-breaking funeral, I began to think about calling off the wedding. August 21 did not seem like a good date, John Wescott did not seem like a good person to marry, and I couldn't see myself in the long white silk gown Mrs. Wescott had offered me. We had gotten engaged at Christmas, while my mother was starting to die; she died in May, earlier than we had expected. When the minister said, "She was a rare spirit, full of the kind of bravery and joy which inspires others," I stared at the pale blue ceiling and thought, "My mother would not have wanted me to spend my life with this man." He had asked me if I wanted him to come to the funeral from Boston, and I said no. And so he didn't, respecting my autonomy and so forth. I think he should have known that I was just being considerate.

After the funeral, we took the little box of ashes back to the house and entertained everybody who came by to pay their respects. Lots of my father's law school colleagues, a few of his former students, my uncle Steve and his new wife, my cousins (whom my sister Lizzie and I always referred to as Thing One and Thing Two), friends from the old neighborhood, before my mother's sculpture started selling, her art world friends, her sisters, some of my friends from high school, some people I used to baby-sit for, my best friend from college, some friends of Lizzie's, a lot of people I didn't recognize. I'd been living away from home for a long time, first at college, now at law school.

My sister, my father, and I worked the room. And everyone who came in my father embraced. It didn't matter whether they started to pat him on the back or shake his hand, he pulled them to him and hugged them so hard I saw people's feet lift right off the floor. Lizzie and I took the more passive route, letting people do whatever they wanted to us, patting, stroking, embracing, cupping our faces in their hands.

My father was in the middle of squeezing Mrs. Ellis, our cleaning lady, when he saw Mr. DeCuervo come in, still carrying his suitcase. He about dropped Mrs. Ellis and went charging over to Mr. DeCuervo, wrapped his arms around him, and the two of them moaned and rocked together in a passionate, musicless waltz. My sister and I sat down on the couch, pressed against each other, watching our father cry all over his friend, our mother's lover.

When I was eleven and Lizzie was eight, her last naked summer, Mr. DeCuervo and his daughter, Gisela, who was just about to turn eight, spent part of the summer with us at the cabin in Maine. The cabin was from the Spencer side, my father's side of the family, and he and my uncle Steve were co-owners. We went there every July (colder water, better weather), and they came in August. My father felt about his

2

brother the way we felt about our cousins, so we would only overlap for lunch on the last day of our stay.

That July, the DeCuervos came, but without Mrs. DeCuervo, who had to go visit a sick someone in Argentina, where they were from. That was okay with us. Mrs. DeCuervo was a professional mother, a type that made my sister and me very uncomfortable. She told us to wash the berries before we ate them, to rest after lunch, to put on more suntan lotion, to make our beds. She was a nice lady, she was just always in our way. My mother had a few very basic summer rules: don't eat food with mold or insects on it; don't swim alone; don't even think about waking your mother before 8:00 A.M. unless you are fatally injured or ill. That was about it, but Mrs. DeCuervo was always amending and adding to the list, one apologetic eye on our mother, who was pleasant and friendly as usual and did things the way she always did. She made it pretty clear that if we were cowed by the likes of Mrs. DeCuervo, we were on our own. They got divorced when Gisela was a sophomore at Mount Holyoke.

We liked pretty, docile Gisela, and bullied her a little bit, and liked her even more because she didn't squeal on us, on me in particular. We liked her father, too. We saw the two of them, sometimes the three of them, at occasional picnics and lesser holidays. He always complimented us, never made stupid jokes at our expense, and brought us unusual, perfect little presents. Silver barrettes for me the summer I was letting my hair grow out from my pixie cut; a leather bookmark for Lizzie, who learned to read when she was three. My mother would stand behind us as we unwrapped the gifts, smiling and shaking her head at his extravagance.

When they drove up, we were all sitting on the porch. Mr. DeCuervo got out first, his curly brown hair making him look like a giant dandelion, with his yellow t-shirt and brown jeans. Gisela looked just like him, her long, curly brown hair caught up in a bun, wisps flying around her tanned little face. As they walked toward us, she took his hand and I felt a rush of warmth for her, for showing how much she loved her daddy, like I loved mine, and for showing that she was a little afraid of us, of me, probably. People weren't often frightened of Lizzie; she never left her books long enough to bother anyone.

My parents came down from the porch; my big father, in his faded blue trunks, drooping below his belly, his freckled back pink and moist in the sun, as it was every summer. The sun caught the red hair on his head and shoulders and chest, and he shone. The Spencers were half-Viking, he said. My mother was wearing her summer outfit, a black two-piece bathing suit. I don't remember her ever wearing a different suit. At night, she'd add one of my father's shirts and wrap it around her like a kimono. Some years, she looked great in her suit, waist nipped in, skin smooth and tan; other years, her skin looked burnt and crumpled, and the suit was too big in some places and too small in others. Those years, she smoked too much and went out on the porch to cough. But that summer the suit fit beautifully, and when she jumped off the porch into my father's arms, he whirled her around and let her black hair whip his face while he smiled and smiled.

They both hugged Mr. DeCuervo and Gisela; my mother took her flowered suitcase and my father took his duffel bag and they led them into the cabin.

The cabin was our palace; Lizzie and I would say very grandly, "We're going to the cabin for the summer, come visit us there, if it's okay with your parents." And we loved it and loved to act as though it was nothing special, when we knew, really, that it was magnificent. The pines and birches came right down to the lake, with just a thin lacing of mossy rocks before you got to the smooth cold water, and little gray fish swam around the splintery dock and through our legs, or out of reach of our oars when we took out the old blue rowboat.

The cabin itself was three bedrooms and a tiny kitchen and a living room that took up half the house. The two small bedrooms had big beds with pastel chenille spreads; yellow with red roses in my parents' room, white with blue pansies in the other. The kids' room was much bigger, like a dormitory, with three sets of bunk beds, each with its own mismatched sheets and pillowcases. The pillows were always a little damp and smelled like salt and pine, and mine smelled of Ma Griffe as well, because I used to sleep with my mother's scarf tucked under it. The shower was outside, with a thin green plastic curtain around it, but there was a regular bathroom inside, next to my parents' room.

Mr. DeCuervo and Gisela fit into our routine as though they'd been coming to the cabin for years, instead of just last summer. We had the kind of summer cabin routine that stays with you forever as a model of leisure, of life being enjoyed. We'd get up early, listening to the birds screaming and trilling, and make ourselves some breakfast; cereal or toast if the parents were up, cake or cold spaghetti or marshmallows if they were still asleep. My mother got up first, usually. She'd make a cup of coffee and brush and braid our hair and set us loose. If we were going exploring, she'd put three sandwiches and three pieces of fruit in a bag, with an army blanket. Otherwise, she'd just wave to us as we headed down to the lake.

We'd come back at lunchtime and eat whatever was around and then go out to the lake or the forest, or down the road to see if the townie kids were in a mood to play with us. I don't know what the grown-ups did all day; sometimes they'd come out to swim for a while, and sometimes we'd find my mother in the shed she used for a studio. But when we came back at five or six, they all seemed happy and relaxed, drinking gin and tonics on the porch, watching us run toward the house. It was the most beautiful time.

At night, after dinner, the fathers would wash up and my mother would sit on the porch, smoking a cigarette, listening to Aretha Franklin or Billie Holiday or Sam Cooke, and after a little while she'd stub out her cigarette and the four of us would dance. We'd twist and lindy and jitterbug and stomp, all of us copying my mother. And pretty soon the daddies would drift in with their dish towels and their beers, and they'd lean in the doorway and watch. My mother would turn first to my father, always to him, first.

"What about it, Danny? Care to dance?" And she'd put her hand on his shoulder and he'd smile, tossing his dish towel to Mr. DeCuervo, resting his beer on the floor. My father would lumber along gamely, shuffling his feet and smiling. Sometimes he'd wave his arms around and pretend to be a fish or a bear while my mother swung her body easily and dreamily, sliding through the music. They'd always lindy together to Fats Domino. That was my father's favorite, and then he'd sit down, puffing a little.

My mother would stand there, snapping her fingers, shifting back and forth.

"Gaucho, you dance with her, before I have a coronary," said my father.

Mr. DeCuervo's real name was Bolivar, which I didn't know until Lizzie told me after the funeral. We always called him

Mr. DeCuervo because we felt embarrassed to call him by a nickname.

So Mr. DeCuervo would shrug gracefully and toss the two dish towels back to my father. And then he'd bop toward my mother, his face still turned toward my father.

"We'll go running tomorrow, Dan, get you back into shape so you can dance all night."

"What do you mean, 'back'? I've been exactly this same svelte shape for twenty years. Why fix it if it ain't broke?"

And they all laughed, and Mr. DeCuervo and my mother rolled their eyes at each other, and my mother walked over and kissed my father where the sweat was beading up at his temples. Then she took Mr. DeCuervo's hand and they walked to the center of the living room.

When she and my father danced, my sister and I giggled and interfered and treated it like a family badminton game in which they were the core players but we were welcome participants. When she danced with Mr. DeCuervo, we'd sit on the porch swing or lean on the windowsill and watch, not even looking at each other.

They only danced the fast dances, and they danced as though they'd been waiting all their lives for each song. My mother's movements got deeper and smoother, and Mr. DeCuervo suddenly came alive, as though a spotlight had hit him. My father danced the way he was, warm, noisy, teasing, a little overpowering; but Mr. DeCuervo, who was usually quiet and thoughtful and serious, became a different man when he danced with my mother. His dancing was light and happy and soulful, edging up on my mother, turning her, matching her every step. They would smile at all of us, in turn, and then face each other, too transported to smile.

"Dance with Daddy some more," my sister said, speaking for all three of us. They had left us too far behind.

My mother blew Lizzie a kiss. "Okay, sweetheart."

She turned to both men, laughing, and said, "That message was certainly loud and clear. Let's take a little break, Gauch, and get these monkeys to bed. It's getting late, girls."

And the three of them shepherded the three of us through the bedtime rituals, moving us in and out of the kitchen for milk, the bathroom for teeth, toilet, and calamine lotion, and finally to our big bedroom. We slept in our underwear and t-shirts, which impressed Gisela.

"No pajamas?" she had said the first night.

"Not necessary," I said smugly.

We would lie there after they kissed us, listening to our parents talk and crack peanuts and snap cards; they played gin and poker while they listened to Dinah Washington and Odetta.

One night, I woke up around midnight and crossed the living room to get some water in the kitchen and see if there was any strawberry shortcake left. I saw my mother and Mr. DeCuervo hugging, and I remember being surprised, and puzzled. I had seen movies; if you hugged someone like you'd never let them go, surely you were supposed to be kissing, too. It wasn't a Mommy-Daddy hug, partly because their hugs were defined by the fact that my father was eight inches taller and a hundred pounds heavier than my mother. These two looked all wrong to me; embraces were a big pink-and-orange man enveloping a small, lean black-and-white woman who gazed up at him. My mother and Mr. DeCuervo looked like sister and brother, standing cheek-to-cheek, with their broad shoulders and long, tanned, bare legs. My mother's hands were under Mr. DeCuervo's white t-shirt.

8

She must have felt my eyes on her, because she opened hers slowly.

"Oh, honey, you startled us. Mr. DeCuervo and I were just saying good night. Do you want me to tuck you in after you go to the bathroom?" Not quite a bribe, certainly a reminder that I was more important to her than he was. They had moved apart so quickly and smoothly I couldn't even remember how they had looked together. I nodded to my mother; what I had seen was already being transformed into a standard good-night embrace, the kind my mother gave to all of her close friends.

When I came back from the bathroom, Mr. DeCuervo had disappeared and my mother was waiting, looking out at the moon. She walked me to the bedroom and kissed me, first on my forehead, then on my lips.

"Sleep well, pumpkin pie. See you in the morning."

"Will you make blueberry pancakes tomorrow?" It seemed like a good time to ask.

"We'll see. Go to sleep."

"Please, Mommy."

"Okay, we'll have a blueberry morning. Go to sleep now. Good night, nurse." And she watched me for a moment from the doorway, and then she was gone.

My father got up at five to go fishing with some men at the other side of the lake. Every Saturday in July he'd go off with a big red bandanna tied over his bald spot, his Mets t-shirt, and his tackle box, and he'd fish until around three. Mr. DeCuervo said that he'd clean them, cook them, and eat them but he wouldn't spend a day with a bunch of guys in baseball caps and white socks to catch them.

I woke up smelling coffee and butter. Gisela and Lizzie were already out of bed, and I was aggrieved; I was the one who had asked for the pancakes, and they were probably all eaten by now.

Mr. DeCuervo and Lizzie were sitting at the table, finishing their pancakes. My mother and Gisela were sitting on the blue couch in the living room while my mother brushed Gisela's hair. She was brushing it more gently than she brushed mine, not slapping her on the shoulder to make her sit still. Gisela didn't wiggle, and she didn't scream when my mother hit a knot.

I was getting ready to be mad when my mother winked at me over Gisela's head and said, "There's a stack of pancakes for you on top of the stove, bunny. Gauch, would you please lift them for Ellen? The plate's probably hot."

Mr. DeCuervo handed me my pancakes, which were huge brown wheels studded with smashed purpley berries; he put my fork and knife on top of a folded paper towel and patted my cheek. His hand smelled like coffee and cinnamon. He knew what I liked and pushed the butter and the honey and the syrup toward me.

"Juice?" he said.

I nodded, trying to watch him when he wasn't looking; he didn't seem like the man I thought I saw in the moonlight, giving my mother a funny hug.

"Great pancakes, Lila," he said.

"Great, Mom." I didn't want to be outclassed by the DeCuervos' habitual good manners. Gisela remembered her "please" and "thank you" for every little thing.

My mother smiled and put a barrette in Gisela's hair. It was starting to get warm, so I swallowed my pancakes and kicked Lizzie to get her attention.

"Let's go," I said.

"Wash your face, then go," my mother said.

I stuck my face under the kitchen tap, and my mother and Mr. DeCuervo laughed. Triumphantly, I led the two little girls out of the house, snatching our towels off the line as we ran down to the water, suddenly filled with longing for the lake.

"Last one in's a fart," I screamed, cannonballing off the end of the dock. I hit the cold blue water, shattering its surface. Lizzie and Gisela jumped in beside me, and we played water games until my father drove up in the pickup with a bucket of fish. He waved to us and told us we'd be eating fish for the next two days, and we groaned and held our noses as he went into the cabin, laughing.

There was a string of sunny days like that one: swimming, fishing with Daddy off the dock, eating peanut butter and jelly sandwiches in the rowboat, drinking Orange Crush on the porch swing.

And then it rained for a week. We woke up the first rainy morning, listening to it tap and dance on the roof. My mother stuck her head into our bedroom.

"It's monsoon weather, honeys. How about cocoa and cinnamon toast?"

We pulled on our overalls and sweaters and went into the kitchen, where my mother had already laid our mugs and plates. She was engaged in her rainy day ritual: making sangria. First she poured the orange juice out of the big white plastic pitcher into three empty peanut butter jars. Then she started chopping up all the oranges, lemons, and limes we had in the house. She let me pour the brandy over the fruit, Gisela threw in the sugar, and Lizzie came up for air long enough to pour the big bottle of red wine over everything. I cannot imagine drinking anything else on rainy days.

My mother went out onto the porch for her morning

cigarette, and when my father came down he joined her while we played Go Fish; I could see them snuggling on the wicker settee. A few minutes later Mr. DeCuervo came down, looked out to the porch, and picked up an old magazine and started reading.

We decided to go play Monopoly in our room since the grown-ups didn't want to entertain us. After two hours, in which I rotted in jail and Lizzie forgot to charge rent, little Gisela beat us and the three of us went back to the kitchen for a snack. Rainy days were basically a series of snacks, more and less elaborate, punctuated by board games, card games, and whining. We drank soda and juice all day, ate cheese, bananas, cookies, bologna, graham crackers, Jiffy popcorn, hard-boiled eggs. The grown-ups ate cheese and crackers and drank sangria.

The daddies were reading in the two big armchairs, my mother had gone off to her room to sketch, and we were getting bored. When my mother came downstairs for a cigarette, I was writing my name in the honey that had spilled on the kitchen table, and Gisela and Lizzie were pulling the stuffing out of the hole in the bottom of the blue couch.

"Jesus Christ, Ellen, get your hands out of the goddamn honey. Liz, Gisela, that's absolutely unacceptable, you know that. Leave the poor couch alone. If you're so damn stir-crazy, go outside and dance in the rain."

The two men looked up, slowly focusing, as if from a great distance.

"Lila, really . . . ," said my father.

"Lila, it's pouring. We'll keep an eye on them now," said Mr. DeCuervo.

"Right. Like you were." My mother was grinning.

"Can we, Mommy, can we go in the rain? Can we take off our clothes and go in the rain?"

"Sure, go naked, there's no point in getting your clothes wet and no point in suits. There's not likely to be a big crowd in the yard."

We raced to the porch before my mother could get rational, stripped and ran whooping into the rain, leaping off the porch onto the muddy lawn, shouting and feeling superior to every child in Maine who had to stay indoors.

We played Goddesses-in-the-Rain, which consisted of caressing our bodies and screaming the names of everyone we knew, and we played ring-around-the-rosy and tag and red light/green light and catch, all deliciously slippery and surreal in the sheets of gray rain. Our parents watched us from the porch.

When we finally came in, thrilled with ourselves and the extent to which we were completely, profoundly wet, in every pore, they bundled us up and told us to dry our hair and get ready for dinner.

My mother brushed our hair, and then she made spaghetti sauce while my father made a salad and Mr. DeCuervo made a strawberry tart, piling the berries into a huge, red, shiny pyramid in the center of the pastry. We were in heaven. The grown-ups were laughing a lot, sipping their rosy drinks, tossing vegetables back and forth.

After dinner, my mother took us into the living room to dance, and then the power went off.

"Shit," said my father in the kitchen.

"Double shit," said Mr. DeCuervo, and we heard them stumbling around in the dark, laughing and cursing, until they came in with two flashlights.

"The cavalry is here, ladies," said Daddy, bowing to us all, twirling his flashlight.

"American and Argentine divisions, señora y señoritas."

I had never heard Mr. DeCuervo speak Spanish before, not even that little bit.

"Well then, I know I'm safe—from the bad guys, anyway. On the other hand . . . " My mother laughed, and the daddies put their arms around each other and they laughed too.

"On the other hand, what? What, Mommy?" I tugged at her the way I did when I was afraid of losing her in a big department store.

"Nothing, honey. Mommy was just being silly. Let's get ready for bed, munchkins. Then you can all talk for a while. We're shut down for the night, I'm sure."

The daddies accompanied us to the bathroom and whispered that we could skip everything except peeing, since there was no electricity. The two of them kissed us good night, my father's mustache tickling, Mr. DeCuervo's sliding over my cheek. My mother came into the room a moment later, and her face was as smooth and warm as a velvet cushion. We didn't stay awake for long. The rain dance and the eating and the storm had worn us out.

It was still dark when I woke up, but the rain had stopped and the power had returned and the light was burning in our hallway. It made me feel very grown-up and responsible, getting out of bed and going around the house, turning out the lights that no one else knew were on; I was conserving electricity.

I went into the bathroom and was squeezed by stomach cramps, probably from all the burnt popcorn kernels I had eaten. I sat on the toilet for a long time, watching a brown spider crawl along the wall; I'd knock him down and then watch him climb back up again, toward the towels. My cramps were better but not gone, so I decided to wake my mother. My father would have been more sympathetic, but he was the heavier sleeper, and by the time he understood what I was telling him, my mother would have her bathrobe on and be massaging my stomach kindly, though without the excited concern I felt was my due as a victim of illness.

I walked down to my parents' room, turning the hall light back on. I pushed open the creaky door and saw my mother spooned up against my father's back, as she always was, and Mr. DeCuervo spooned up against her, his arm over the covers, his other hand resting on the top of her head.

I stood and looked and then backed out of the bedroom. They hadn't moved, the three of them breathing deeply, in unison. What was that, I thought, what did I see? I wanted to go back and take another look, to see it again, to make it disappear, to watch them carefully, until I understood.

My cramps were gone. I went back to my own bed, staring at Lizzie and Gisela, who looked in their sleep like little girl-versions of the two men I had just seen. Just sleeping, I thought, the grown-ups were just sleeping. Maybe Mr. DeCuervo's bed had collapsed, like ours did two summers ago. Or maybe it got wet in the storm. I thought I would never be able to fall asleep, but the next thing I remember is waking up to more rain and Lizzie and Gisela begging my mother to take us to the movies in town. We went to see *The Sound of Music,* which had been playing at the Bijou for about ten years.

I don't remember much else about the summer; all of the images run together. We went on swimming and fishing and taking the rowboat out for little adventures, and when the DeCuervos left I hugged Gisela but wasn't going to hug him, until he whispered in my ear, "Next year we'll bring up a motorboat and I'll teach you to water ski," and then I hugged him very hard and my mother put her hand on my head lightly, giving benediction.

The next summer, I went off to camp in July and wasn't there when the DeCuervos came. Lizzie said they had a good time without me. Then they couldn't come for a couple of summers in a row, and by the time they came again, Gisela and Lizzie were at camp with me in New Hampshire; the four grown-ups spent about a week together, and later I heard my father say that another vacation with Elvira DeCuervo would kill him, or he'd kill her. My mother said she wasn't so bad.

We saw them a little less after that. They came, Gisela and Mr. DeCuervo, to my high school graduation, to my mother's opening in Boston, my father's fiftieth birthday party, and then Lizzie's graduation. When my mother went down to New York she'd have dinner with the three of them, she said, but sometimes her plans would change and they'd have to substitute lunch for dinner.

Gisela couldn't come to the funeral. She was in Argentina for the year, working with the architectural firm that Mr. DeCuervo's father had started.

After all the mourners left, Mr. DeCuervo gave us a sympathy note from Gisela, with a beautiful pen-and-ink of our mother inside it. The two men went into the living room and took out a bottle of Scotch and two glasses. It was like we weren't there; they put on Billie Holiday singing "Embraceable You," and they got down to serious drinking and grieving. Lizzie and I went into the kitchen and decided to eat everything sweet that people had brought over: brownies, strudel, pfeffernuesse, sweet potato pie, Mrs. Ellis's chocolate cake with chocolate mousse in the middle. We laid out two plates and two mugs of milk and got to it.

Lizzie said, "You know, when I was home in April, he called every day." She jerked her head toward the living room.

I couldn't tell if she approved or disapproved, and I didn't know what I thought about it either.

"She called him Bolivar."

"What? She always called him Gaucho, and so we didn't call him anything."

"I know, but she called him Bolivar. I heard her talking to him every fucking day, El, she called him Bolivar."

Tears were running down Lizzie's face, and I wished my mother was there to pat her soft fuzzy hair and keep her from choking on her tears. I held her hand across the table, still holding my fork in my other hand. I could feel my mother looking at me, smiling and narrowing her eyes a little, the way she did when I was balking. I dropped the fork onto my plate and went over and hugged Lizzie, who leaned into me as though her spine had collapsed.

"I asked her about it after the third call," she said into my shoulder.

"What'd she say?" I straightened Lizzie up so I could hear her.

"She said, 'Of course he calls at noon. He knows that's when I'm feeling strongest.' And I told her that's not what I meant, that I hadn't known they were so close."

"You said that?"

"Yeah. And she said, 'Honey, nobody loves me more than Bolivar.' And I didn't know what to say, so I just sat there feeling like 'Do I really want to hear this?' and then she fell asleep."

"So what do you think?"

"I don't know. I was getting ready to ask her again—"

"You're amazing, Lizzie," I interrupted. She really is, she's so quiet, but she goes and has conversations I can't even imagine having.

17

"But I didn't have to ask because she brought it up herself, the next day after he called. She got off the phone, looking just so exhausted, she was sweating but she was smiling. She was staring out at the crab apple trees in the yard, and she said, 'There were apple trees in bloom when I met Bolivar, and the trees were right where the sculpture needed to be in the courtyard, and so he offered to get rid of the trees and I said that seemed arrogant and he said that they'd replant them. So I said, "Okay," and he said, "What's so bad about arrogance?" And the first time he and Daddy met, the two of them drank Scotch and watched soccer while I made dinner. And then they washed up, just like at the cabin. And when the two of them are in the room together and you two girls are with us, I know that I am living in a state of grace.'"

"She said that? She said 'in a state of grace'? Mommy said that?"

"Yes, Ellen. Christ, what do you think, I'm making up interesting deathbed statements?" Lizzie hates to be interrupted, especially by me.

"Sorry. Go on."

"Anyway, we were talking and I sort of asked what were we actually talking about. I mean, close friends or very close friends, and she just laughed. You know how she'd look at us like she knew exactly where we were going when we said we were going to a friend's house for the afternoon but we were really going to drink Boone's Farm and skinny-dip at the quarry? Well, she looked just like that and she took my hand. Her hand was so light, El. And she said that the three of them loved each other, each differently, and that they were both amazing men, each special, each deserving love and appreciation. She said that she thought Daddy was the most wonderful

husband a woman could have and that she was very glad we
had him as a father. And I asked her how she could do it, love
them both, and how they could stand it. And she said, 'Love is
not a pie, honey. I love you and Ellen differently because you
are different people, wonderful people, but not at all the same.
And so who I am with each of you is different, unique to us. I
don't choose between you. And it's the same way with Daddy
and Bolivar. People think that it can't be that way, but it can.
You just have to find the right people.' And then she shut her
eyes for the afternoon. Your eyes are bugging out, El."

"Well, Jesus, I guess so. I mean, I knew . . . "

"You knew? And you didn't tell me?"

"You were eight or something, Lizzie, what was I supposed
to say? I didn't even know what I knew then."

"So, what did you know?" Lizzie was very serious. It was a
real breach of our rules not to share inside dirt about our parents, especially our mother; we were always trying to figure
her out.

I didn't know how to tell her about the three of them; that
was even less normal than her having an affair with Mr.
DeCuervo with Daddy's permission. I couldn't even think of the
words to describe what I had seen, so I just said, "I saw Mommy
and Mr. DeCuervo kissing one night after we were in bed."

"Really? Where was Daddy?"

"I don't know. But wherever he was, obviously he knew
what was going on. I mean, that's what Mommy was telling
you, right? That Daddy knew and that it was okay with him."

"Yeah. Jesus."

I went back to my chair and sat down. We were halfway
through the strudel when the two men came in. They were
drunk but not incoherent. They just weren't their normal

selves, but I guess we weren't either, with our eyes puffy and red and all this destroyed food around us.

"Beautiful girls," Mr. DeCuervo said to my father. They were hanging in the doorway, one on each side.

"They are, they really are. And smart, couldn't find smarter girls."

My father went on and on about how smart we were. Lizzie and I just looked at each other, embarrassed but not displeased.

"Ellen has Lila's mouth," Mr. DeCuervo said. "You have your mother's mouth, with the right side going up a little more than the left. Exquisite."

My father was nodding his head, like this was the greatest truth ever told. And Daddy turned to Lizzie and said, "And you have your mother's eyes. Since the day you were born and I looked right into them, I thought, 'My God, she's got Lila's eyes, but blue, not green.'"

And Mr. DeCuervo was nodding away, of course. I wondered if they were going to do a complete autopsy, but they stopped.

My father came over to the table and put one hand on each of us. "You girls made your mother incredibly happy. There was nothing she ever created that gave her more pride and joy than you two. And she thought that you were both so special . . . " He started crying, and Mr. DeCuervo put an arm around his waist and picked up for him.

"She did, she had two big pictures of you in her studio, nothing else. And you know, she expected us all to grieve, but you know how much she wanted you to enjoy, too. To enjoy everything, every meal, every drink, every sunrise, every kiss . . . " He started crying too.

"We're gonna lie down for a while, girls. Maybe later we'll

have dinner or something." My father kissed us both, wet and rough, and the two of them went down the hall.

Lizzie and I looked at each other again.

"Wanna get drunk?" I said.

"No, I don't think so. I guess I'll go lie down for a while too, unless you want company." She looked like she was about to sleep standing up, so I shook my head. I was planning on calling John anyway.

Lizzie came over and hugged me, hard, and I hugged her back and brushed the chocolate crumbs out of her hair.

Sitting alone in the kitchen, I thought about John, about telling him about my mother and her affair and how the two men were sacked out in my parents' bed, probably snoring. And I could hear John's silence and I knew that he would think my father must not have really loved my mother if he'd let her go with another man; or that my mother must have been a real bitch, forcing my father to tolerate an affair "right in his own home," John would think, maybe even say. I thought I ought to call him before I got myself completely enraged over a conversation that hadn't taken place. Lizzie would say I was projecting anyway.

I called, and John was very sweet, asking how I was feeling, how the memorial service had gone, how my father was. And I told him all that and then I knew I couldn't tell him the rest and that I couldn't marry a man I couldn't tell this story to.

"I'm so sorry, Ellen," he said. "You must be very upset. What a difficult day for you."

I realize that was a perfectly normal response, it just was all wrong for me. I didn't come from a normal family, I wasn't ready to get normal.

I felt terrible, hurting John, but I couldn't marry him just because I didn't want to hurt him, so I said, "And that's not the worst of it, John. I can't marry you, I really can't. I know this is pretty hard to listen to over the phone. . . ." I couldn't think what else to say.

"Ellen, let's talk about this when you get back to Boston. I know what kind of a strain you must be under. I had the feeling that you were unhappy about some of Mother's ideas. We can work something out when you get back."

"I know you think this is because of my mother's death, and it is, but not the way you think. John, I just can't marry you. I'm not going to wear your mother's dress and I'm not going to marry you and I'm very sorry."

He was quiet for a long time, and then he said, "I don't understand, Ellen. We've already ordered the invitations." And I knew that I was right. If he had said, "Fuck this, I'm coming to see you tonight," or even, "I don't know what you're talking about, but I want to marry you anyway," I'd probably have changed my mind before I got off the phone. But as it was, I said good-bye sort of quietly and hung up.

It was like two funerals in one day. I sat at the table, poking the cake into little shapes and then knocking them over. My mother would have sent me out for a walk. I'd started clearing the stuff away when my father and Mr. DeCuervo appeared, looking more together.

"How about some gin rummy, El?" my father said.

"If you're up for it," said Mr. DeCuervo.

"Okay," I said. "I just broke up with John Wescott."

"Oh?"

I couldn't tell which one spoke.

"I told him that I didn't think we'd make each other happy."

Which was what I had meant to say.

My father hugged me and said, "I'm sorry that it's hard for

you. You did the right thing." Then he turned to Mr. DeCuervo and said, "Did she know how to call them, or what? Your mother knew that you weren't going to marry that guy."

"She was almost always right, Dan."

"Almost always, not quite," said my father, and the two of them laughed at some private joke and shook hands like a pair of old boxers.

"So, you deal," my father said, leaning back in his chair.

"Penny a point," said Mr. DeCuervo.

Song of Solomon

Kate stood in front of the mirror trying on dresses. She could almost get into her black suit, but that couldn't be right for the New Year and it was almost eighty outside. She put on a yellow sleeveless dress with a white linen blazer and white sandals. Too summery but not bizarre. Do they wear hats? In church, women wear hats. Do Jewish women wear hats? Kate stared into the mirror, sweating in her slip, milk starting to come through her nursing pads.

Not now, she thought. If I nurse the baby, I'll be late for the ceremony—no, the services. Be calm, you must nurse the baby, Dr. Sheldon would want you to nurse the baby, you can tell him that you were almost late because you had to nurse Sarah and he'll smile. Kate relaxed, thinking of his smile, like a cool cloth on her cheek.

Okay, we're all right. Kate took off her yellow dress, laid it out, and called to Sarah, who was just starting to make her little sucking noises, "It's okay, Mommy's coming, everything's okay." On her way to the baby's room, she grabbed a towel and looked on the top shelf of the closet for her white cartwheel straw hat. God did love her. He knew she had to get to the temple. The hat was there, and it was unblemished and unbent.

Kate looked at Sarah and felt the milk slide under her bra, down her rib cage. "Here we are, little duck. Mommy's baby. Dr. Sheldon's perfect girl." She picked Sarah up and changed her, watching herself move smoothly and competently, like a Pampers commercial. Sarah didn't wiggle, just knotted her toes in Kate's long blond hair. She plunked down in the rocking chair with Sarah and nursed her, wincing for a second as that ruthless, sweet mouth clamped down on her nipple. She watched Sarah and she watched the clock.

"Okay, Sarah beans, ten on one, ten on the other, and then we're out of here. Going to temple. Going out today, Miss Sarah." While Sarah took a short break between breasts, Kate grabbed a clean blue dress from the laundry basket and put Sarah into it.

We're almost there, Kate thought. Come on, plan ahead. Plan it so you don't screw up. Okay, she finishes nursing, I burp her, on the towel. I put her in her crib while I get dressed, my shoes are not in my closet, they're still in the hall closet. Okay, we're walking down the hall—no, the diaper bag. The diaper bag is in Sarah's room and it's already packed, with another dress. Good girl, Kate. Okay, we have a fed baby, a diaper bag, a dressed mother. The hat, the hat is still in the closet, you don't put it on until you get there and you can see what they wear.

Make-up. You put your make-up in your purse, your white purse sitting on the hall bench, ready to roll. All you need is a little lip gloss and some cover-up for your raccoon eyes. You're all right. He doesn't care for make-up. Remember, in the hospital, sitting on your bed, he said that he didn't care for make-up and that you didn't need it anyway.

Kate closed her eyes, to remember better what he said, his saying it, to feel the weight of his body at the end of the bed, her bare feet almost touching his hip.

The whole seventy-two hours in the hospital Kate's body was never dry. She was damp and awake for every sunrise, her wet nightgown twisted up around her waist. Blood, milk, and sweat streamed over and through her. The night nurse had told her to get up and walk, but she was terrified that when she stood up her organs would just fall out, the cut muscles and tissue crumbling away like rotted newspaper.

"I promise you, you start walking now, when all the other ladies are home taking Percoset you'll be pushing Miss Sarah around the block. I'll take that catheter out now, too."

She saw the nurse's smooth, thick hands flick back the heavy hem of her nightgown, and she shut her eyes when she felt the slight emptying tug.

"All right, let's roll."

Let's roll, Kate thought, and stood up, wanting her voice to match the nurse's light bounce. Let's roll on out of here. She could hear the crowds cheering in her head as she walked down the hall, the i.v. rack skittering alongside her, the nurse's hand gently pulling on her good arm. She felt the shimmery heat of his presence before she really saw him, his back to her, talking to the nurses at the coffee station. They were barricaded behind twin coffeepots, personalized mugs, wide open doughnut boxes.

Kate shook off her nurse and strolled, with great effort, toward the coffee station.

"Wonderful. You're walking already, isn't that wonderful?" Dr. Sheldon turned to the nurses, who smiled politely; they didn't care if she walked or not, and Kate didn't care about them either. If she didn't say something, he'd be gone, and she was too tired to stand around waiting for the right moment.

"Could I speak to you?" The sweat slid from her underarms right down to her feet, wetting the paper slippers they'd given her.

"Of course. I'll save your nurse a trip, even if your quality of care suffers a little."

The nurses all smiled; he was a corny old guy, but nice. He practically lived in the maternity ward. His patient, the new mother, looked like she was about to pass out, and Kate's nurse went to grab a cup of coffee before the inevitable call.

He put his hand around her bicep, and Kate could feel the blood rushing from her arm to her cheeks.

"The nurses like you," she said, looking at the passing room numbers so he couldn't see her face.

"Yes? I like them. It's hard work, they're terribly understaffed. First there weren't enough nurses because they were paid so badly. Now there aren't enough nurses because it costs the hospitals too much to keep a full shift."

Kate smiled. Even though her back ached and she could picture each of her twenty stitches clearly, lighting a hot, narrow torch across her belly, she beamed. He gripped her arm a little tighter, and as her face went white and the walls around Dr. Sheldon began to spin, she smiled again and he smiled back before he called the nurse.

Sarah had stopped sucking a little sooner than usual, and Kate was so grateful she sang to her all the way through burping. Everything went smoothly; little Sarah, stoned from nursing, was completely content to lie in her crib and murmur to the world. Kate dressed like a surgeon prepping, precise and careful in every movement. She checked her watch again. Twenty-five minutes to get to the temple. She had driven there yesterday and timed it; it was only fifteen minutes away. Five minutes to find a parking space, five minutes to get Sarah out of her NASA-designed carseat and into her Snugli. Forget the Snugli, in a summer dress and a blazer you can't carry a baby in a blue corduroy Snugli. Okay, no Snugli. I carry her in my arms, wrapped in a yellow and blue blanket, to show off her eyes and her hair. Fine.

Kate moved through all of her steps, locked the front door, and got into the car, strapping Sarah in with the blanket tucked around her, supporting her soft boneless neck.

"We're rolling now. Off we go, into the wild blue yonder, flying high into the sky . . . " Sarah had fallen into one of her instant naps, from which she would emerge charming and alert but not yet hungry. Perfect for seeing Dr. Sheldon.

Kate didn't even look pregnant until her sixth month. The other women in the library began to talk to her a little, to tell her things. They had left her alone all summer, feeling that whether her silence was due to a bad attitude, problems at home, or painful shyness, she was too much trouble. Pregnant and single and willing to take anyone's advice, Kate was not too much trouble. "Go to Dr. Sheldon," they said over lunch in the back room. "He's the best." Especially for the weird, the dispossessed, the single mothers, the ones who wished they were, the ones who needed to talk at two in the morning, not just about their babies. And when Kate met Dr. Sheldon and he didn't purse his lips when she said she had only met the father once and hoped she never would again, she knew that she and the baby were in the right place. When he helped her out of her chair, she felt ethereally beautiful and as delicate as baby's breath, her ankles and heartburn forgotten.

She drove up to the synagogue and was appalled to see millions of cars. It looked like an airport terminal, women and children piling out of backseats, all the women wearing hats. Kate laid her hand happily on the white hat next to her, perfect for her blond hair. He'd like it. She could tell he liked her hair from the way he commented on Sarah's duck fuzz. "Not much now," he said the night he sat so close to her, "but she'll have your curls by the time she's one." The men were pulling away from the entrance, craning their necks to find parking spaces. They weren't wearing hats, of course, just those little beanies— what were they called? She could ask Dr. Sheldon. Unless he'd be offended by her ignorance, rather than charmed by her interest? Please let him find me charming, and my daughter irresistible.

She was damp and rumpled by the time she found a spot behind the A&P. She scooped up Sarah like she was going for a touchdown and trotted toward the temple, hugely domed and out of scale between a sandwich shop and a dry cleaners. A block away, Kate slowed down, licked her lips, and smoothed the front of her dress with her free hand. Please.

He was standing on the sidewalk talking to some other men, but alone. No wife. She would put one of those St. Jude ads in the paper, the kind that said, "Thank you for helping me. Now I need you more than ever." She shifted Sarah to her left shoulder, lined up her purse and the diaper bag on her right shoulder, and smiled the way her mother had always wanted her to.

"Why, Dr. Sheldon."

"Ms. Tillinghast. What a surprise, what a pleasure. I didn't know we belonged to the same shul."

Kate thought quickly, circling the strange word. "I've never been here before, actually, but I've wanted to come for a long time. I hope nobody will mind the baby, my regular sitter couldn't make it." Kate smiled self-deprecatingly, showing that she knew some people didn't like babies and would consider her careless for having brought Sarah. But Dr. Sheldon wouldn't think so, which was why she had told Joan not to come today.

"No, of course not. Who could object to this angel, this proof of God's goodness?"

As he bent his head toward Sarah to kiss the back of her round moist head, Kate felt so happy she thought her heart would break through her chest and fly around the temple, like a dove released.

They squinted at each other in the September light, smiling and wondering what the other person saw. Dr. Sheldon thought Kate saw a pallid, overweight man sweating in an old navy blue suit, black-rimmed glasses sliding halfway down his big nose and wild gray curls floating around his bald spot. She didn't; she saw God. Kate thought he saw a slightly crazy woman, wild with exhaustion and loneliness, but he didn't see that. He saw that her dark blue eyes lit up when they rested on his face and that her hand lay tenderly, unconsciously, on his sleeve, like a lily. He saw that their house would have white flowers and bright plastic toys on the floor. He would not be alone.

"People are starting to go in," he said.

"Oh." She sounded wounded, which alarmed him. Had he offended her? Maybe she didn't want to sit with him.

Dr. Sheldon shuffled backward, to show that he hadn't meant to intrude, and Kate's eyes filled with tears. How could he be leaving now, now that they were together?

Sarah thrust one pink foot through her blanket, and they both looked at it, flexing in the air. Kate's face was so filled with loss and love that Dr. Sheldon reached out for her, and she pressed his hand to her hip as they carried Sarah up the temple stairs.

Sleepwalking

I was born smart and had been lucky my whole life, so I didn't even know that what I thought was careful planning was nothing more than being in the right place at the right time, missing the avalanche that I didn't even hear.

After the funeral was over and the cold turkey and the glazed ham were demolished and some very good jazz was played and some very good musicians went home drunk on bourbon poured in Lionel's honor, it was just me, my mother-in-law, Ruth, and the two boys, Lionel Junior from Lionel's second marriage and our little boy, Buster.

Ruth pushed herself up out of the couch, her black taffeta dress rustling reproachfully. I couldn't stand for her to start the dishes, sighing, praising the Lord, clucking her tongue over the state of my kitchen, in which the windows are not washed regularly and I do not scrub behind the refrigerator.

"Ruth, let them sit. I'll do them later tonight."

"No need to put off 'til tomorrow what we can do today. I'll do them right now, and then Lionel Junior can run me home." Ruth does not believe that the good Lord intended ladies to drive; she'd drive, eyes closed, with her drunk son or her accident-prone grandson before she'd set foot in my car.

"Ruth, please, I'd just as soon have something to do later. Please. Let me make us a cup of tea, and then we'll take you home."

Tea, Buster, and Lionel's relative sobriety were the three major contributions I'd made to Ruth's life; the tea and Buster accounted for all of our truces and the few good times we'd had together.

"I ought to be going along now, let you get on with things."

"Earl Grey? Darjeeling? Constant Comment? I've got some rosehip tea in here too, it's light, sort of lemony." I don't know why I was urging her to stay, I'd never be rid of her as long as I had the boys. If Ruth no longer thought I was trash, she certainly made it clear that I hadn't lived up to her notion of the perfect daughter-in-law, a cross between Marian Anderson and Florence Nightingale.

"You have Earl Grey?" Ruth was wavering, half a smile on her sad mouth, her going-to-church lipstick faded to a blurry pink line on her upper lip.

When I really needed Ruth on my side, I'd set out an English tea: Spode teapot, linen place mats, scones, and three kinds of jam. And for half an hour, we'd sip and chew, happy to be so civilized.

"Earl Grey it is." I got up to put on the water, stepping on Buster who was sitting on the floor by my chair, practically on my feet.

"Jesus, Buster, are you all right?" I hugged him before he could start crying and lifted him out of my way.

"The Lord's Name," Ruth murmured, rolling her eyes up to apologize to Jesus personally. I felt like smacking her one, right in her soft dark face, and pointing out that since the Lord had not treated us especially well in the last year, during which we had both lost husbands, perhaps we didn't have to be overly concerned with His hurt feelings. Ruth made me want to become a spectacularly dissolute pagan.

"Sorry, Ruth. Buster, sit down by your grandmother, honey, and I'll make us all some tea."

"No, really, don't trouble yourself, Julia. Lionel Junior, please take me home. Gabriel, come kiss your grandma good-bye. You boys be good, now, and think of how your daddy would want you to act. I'll see you all for dinner tomorrow."

She was determined to leave, martyred and tea-less, so I got on line to kiss her. Ruth put her hands on my shoulders, her only gesture of affection toward me, which also allowed her to pretend that she was a little taller, rather than a little shorter, than I am.

She left with the Lion, and Buster and I cuddled on the couch, his full face squashed against my chest, my skin resting on his soft hair. I felt almost whole.

"Sing, Mama."

Lionel always wanted me to record with him and I always said no, because I don't like performing and I didn't want to be a blues-singing Marion Davies to Lionel's William Randolph Hearst. But I loved to sing and he loved to play and I'm sorry we didn't record just one song together.

I was trying to think of something that would soothe Buster but not break my heart.

I sang "Amazing Grace," even though I can't quite hit that note, and I sang bits and pieces of a few more songs, and then Buster was asleep and practically drowning in my tears.

I heard Lionel Junior's footsteps and blotted my face on my sleeve.

"Hey, Lion, let's put this little boy to bed."

"He's out, huh? You look tired too. Why don't you go to bed and I'll do the dishes?"

That's my Lion. I think because I chose to love him, chose to be a mother and not just his father's wife, Lion gave me back everything he could. He was my table setter, car washer, garden weeder; in twelve years, I might've raised my voice to him twice. When Lionel brought him to meet me the first time, I looked into those wary eyes, hope pouring out of them despite himself, and I knew that I had found someone else to love.

I carried Buster to his room and laid him on the bed, slipping off his loafers. I pulled up the comforter with the long-legged basketball players running all over it and kissed his damp little face. I thought about how lucky I was to have Buster and Lion and even Ruth, who might torture me forever but would never abandon me, and I thought about how cold and lonely my poor Lionel must be, with no bourbon and no music and no audience, and I went into the bathroom to dry my face again. Lion got frantic when he saw me crying.

He was lying on the couch, his shoes off, his face turned toward the cushions.

"Want a soda or a beer? Maybe some music?"

"Nope. Maybe some music, but not Pop's."

"No, no, not your father's. How about Billie Holiday, Sarah Vaughan?"

"How about something a little more up? How about Luther Vandross?" He had turned around to face me.

"I don't have any—as you know." Lionel and I both hated bubble-gum music, so of course Lion had the world's largest collection of whipped-cream soul; if it was insipid, he bought it.

"I'll get my tapes," he said, and sat halfway up to see if I would let him. We used to make him play them in his room so we wouldn't have to listen, but Lionel wasn't here to grumble at the boy and I just didn't care.

"Play what you want, honey," I said, sitting in Lionel's brown velvet recliner. Copies of *Downbeat* and packs of Trident were still stuffed between the cushion and the arm. Lion bounded off to his room and came back with an armful of tapes.

"Luther Vandross, Whitney Houston . . . what would you like to hear?"

"You pick." Even talking felt like too much work. He put on one of the tapes and I shut my eyes.

I hadn't expected to miss Lionel so much. We'd had twelve years together, eleven of them sober; we'd had Buster and raised the Lion, and we'd gone to the Grammys together when he was nominated and he'd stayed sober when he lost, and we'd made love, with more interest some years than others; we'd been through a few other women for him, a few blondes that he couldn't pass up, and one other man for me, so I'm not criticizing him. We knew each other so well that when I wrote a piece on another jazz musician, he'd find the one phrase and say, "You meant that about me," and he'd be right. He was a better father than your average musician; he'd bring us with him whenever he went to Europe, and no matter how late he played on Saturday, he got up and made breakfast on Sunday.

Maybe we weren't a perfect match, in age, or temperament, or color, but we did try and we were willing to stick it out and then we didn't get a chance.

Lion came and sat by me, putting his head against my knee. Just like Buster, I thought. Lion's mother was half-Italian, like me, so the two boys look alike: creamier, silkier versions of their father.

I patted his hair and ran my thumb up and down his neck, feeling the muscles bunched up. When he was little, he couldn't fall asleep without his nightly back rub, and he only gave it up when he was fifteen and Lionel just wouldn't let me anymore.

"It's midnight, honey. It's been a long day, a long week. Go to bed."

He pushed his head against my leg and cried, the way men do, like it's being torn out of them. His tears ran down my bare leg, and I felt the strings holding me together just snap. One, two, three, and there was no more center.

"Go to bed, Lion."

"How about you?"

"I'm not really ready for bed yet, honey. Go ahead." Please, go to bed.

"Okay. Good night, Ma."

"Good night, baby." Nineteen-year-old baby.

He pulled himself up and went off to his room. I peered into the kitchen, looked at all the dishes, and closed my eyes again. After a while, I got up and finished off the little bit of Jim Beam left in the bottle. With all Lionel's efforts at sobriety, we didn't keep the stuff around, and I choked on it. But the burning in my throat was comforting, like old times, and it was a distraction.

I walked down the hall to the bedroom, I used to call it the Lionel Sampson Celebrity Shrine. It wasn't just his framed album covers, but all of his favorite reviews, including the ones I wrote before I met him; one of Billie's gardenias mounted on velvet, pressed behind glass; photos of Lionel playing with equally famous or more famous musicians or with famous fans. In some ways, it's easier to marry a man with a big ego; you're not always fretting over him, worrying about whether or not he needs fluffing up.

I threw my black dress on the floor, my worst habit, and got into bed. I woke up at around four, waiting for something. A minute later, Buster wandered in, eyes half-shut, blue blankie resurrected and hung around his neck, like a little boxer.

"Gonna stay with you, Mama." Truculent even in his sleep, knowing that if his father had been there, he'd have been sent back to his own room.

"Come in, then, Bus. Let's try and get some sleep."

He curled up next to me, silently, an arm flung over me, the other arm thrust into his pajama bottoms, between his legs.

I had just shut my eyes again when I felt something out of place. Lion was standing in the doorway, his briefs hanging off his high skinny hips. He needed new underwear, I thought. He looked about a year older than Buster.

"I thought I heard Buster prowling around, y'know, sleep-walking."

The only one who ever sleepwalked in our family was Lion, but I didn't say so. "It's okay, he just wanted company. Lonely in this house tonight."

"Yeah. Ma?"

I was tired of thinking, and I didn't want to send him away, and I didn't want to talk anymore to anyone so I said, "Come on, honey, it's a big bed."

He crawled in next to his brother and fell asleep in a few minutes. I watched the digital clock flip through a lot of numbers and finally I got up and read.

The boys woke early, and I made them what Lionel called a Jersey City breakfast: eggs, sweet Italian sausage, grits, biscuits, and a quart of milk for each of them.

"Buster, soccer camp starts today. Do you feel up to going?"

I didn't see any reason for him to sit at home; he could catch up on his grieving for the rest of his life.

"I guess so. Is it okay, Mama?"

"Yes, honey, it's fine. I'm glad you're going. I'll pick you up at five, and then we'll drive straight over to Grandma's for dinner. You go get ready when you're done eating. Don't forget your cleats, they're in the hall."

Lion swallowed his milk and stood up, like a brown flamingo, balancing on one foot while he put on his sneaker. "Come on, Buster, I'm taking you, I have to go into town anyway. Do we need anything?"

I hadn't been to the grocery store in about a week. "Get milk and o.j. and English muffins and American cheese. I'll do a real shop tomorrow." If I could just get to the store and the cleaners, then I could get to work, and then my life would move forward.

Finally they were ready to go, and I kissed them both and gave Lion some money for the groceries.

"I'll be back by lunchtime," he said. It was already eight-thirty. Since his father got sick, he'd been giving me hourly bulletins on his whereabouts. That summer, he was house-painting and was home constantly, leaving late, back early, stopping by for lunch.

"If you like," I said. I didn't want him to feel that he had to keep me company. I was planning on going back to work tomorrow or the day after.

While the boys were gone, I straightened the house, went for a walk, and made curried tuna fish sandwiches for Lion. I watched out the window for him, and when I saw my car turn up the road, I remembered all the things I hadn't done and started making a list. He came in, sweating and shirtless, drops of white paint on his hands and shoulders and sneakers.

Lion ate and I watched him and smiled. Feeding them was the easiest and clearest way of loving them, holding them.

"I'm going to shower. Then we could play a little tennis or work on the porch." He finished both sandwiches in about a minute and got that wistful look that teenage boys get when they want you to fix them something more to eat. I made two peanut butter and jelly sandwiches and put them on his plate.

"Great. I don't have to work this afternoon. I told Joe I might not be back, he said okay."

"Well, I'm just going to mouse around, do laundry, answer some mail. I'm glad to have your company, you know I am, but you don't have to stay here with me. You might want to be with your friends."

"I don't. I'm gonna shower." Like his father, he only put his love out once, and God help you if you didn't take the hint.

I sat at the table, looking out at the morning glories climbing up the trellis Lionel had built me the summer he stopped drinking. In addition to the trellis, I had two flower boxes, a magazine rack, and a footstool so ugly even Ruth wouldn't have it.

"Ma, no towels," Lion shouted from the bathroom. I thought that was nice, as if real life might continue.

"All right," I called, getting one of the big, rough white ones that he liked.

I went into the bathroom and put it on the rack just as he stepped out of the shower. I hadn't seen him naked since he was fourteen and spent the year parading around the house topless, so that we could admire his underarm hair and the little black wisps between his nipples.

All I could see in the mist was a dark caramel column and two patches of dark curls, inky against his skin. I expected him to look away, embarrassed, but instead he looked right at me as he took the towel, and I was the one who turned away.

"Sorry," we both said, and I backed out of the bathroom and went straight down to the basement so we wouldn't bump into each other for a while.

I washed, dried, and folded everything that couldn't get away from me, listening for Lion's footsteps upstairs. I couldn't hear anything while the machines were going, so after about an hour I came up and found a note on the kitchen table.

"Taking a nap. Wake me when it's time to get Buster. L."

"L." is how his father used to sign his notes. And their handwriting was the same too: the awkward careful printing of men who know that their script is illegible.

I took a shower and dried my hair and looked in the mirror for a while, noticing the gray at the temples. I wondered what Lion would have seen if he'd walked in on me, and I decided not to ever think like that again.

I woke Lion by calling him from the hall, then I went into my room while he dressed to go to his grandmother's. I found a skirt that was somber and ill-fitting enough to meet Ruth's standard of widowhood and thought about topping it off with my "Eight to the Bar Volleyball Champs" t-shirt, but didn't. Even pulling Ruth's chain wasn't fun. I put on a yellow shirt that made me look like one of the Neapolitan cholera victims, and Lion and I went to get Buster. He was bubbling over the goal he had made in the last quarter, and that filled the car until we got to Ruth's house, and then she took over.

"Come in, come in. Gabriel, you are too dirty to be my grandson. You go wash up right now. Lionel Junior, you're

42

looking a little peaked. You must be working too hard or playing too hard. Does he eat, Julia? Come sit down here and have
a glass of nice iced tea with mint from my garden. Julia, guess
who I heard from this afternoon? Loretta, Lionel's first wife?
She called to say how sorry she was. I told her she could call
upon you, if she wished."

"Fine." I didn't have the energy to be annoyed. My muscles
felt like butter, I'd had a headache for six days, and my
eyes were so sore that even when I closed them, they ached. If
Ruth wanted to sic Loretta McVay Sampson de Guzman de
God-knows-who-else on me, I guessed I'd get through that little hell too.

Ruth looked at me, probably disappointed; I knew from
Lionel that she couldn't stand Loretta, but since she was the
only black woman he'd married, Ruth felt obliged to find
something positive about her. She was a lousy singer, a whore,
and a terrible housekeeper, so Ruth really had to search. Anita,
wife number two, was a rich, pretty flake with a fragile air and
a serious drug problem that killed her when the Lion was five. I
was the only normal, functioning person he was ever involved
with: I worked, I cooked, I balanced our checkbook, I did what
had to be done, just like Ruth. And I irritated her no end.

"Why'd you do that, Grandma? Loretta's so nasty. She
probably just wants to find out if Pop left her something in his
will, which I'm sure he did not." Loretta and Lionel had a little thing going when Anita was in one of her rehab centers,
and I think the Lion found out and of course blamed Loretta.

"It's all right, Lion," I said, and stopped myself from patting
his hand as if he was Buster.

Ruth was offended. "Really, young man, it was very decent,
just common courtesy, for Loretta to pay her respects, and I'm
sure that your stepmother appreciates that." Ruth thought it

disrespectful to call me Julia when talking to Lion, but she couldn't stand the fact that he called me Ma after the four years she put in raising him while Anita killed herself and Lionel toured. So she'd refer to me as "your stepmother," which always made me feel like the coachmen and pumpkins couldn't be far behind. Lion used to look at me and smile when she said it.

We got through dinner, with Buster bragging about soccer and giving us a minute-by-minute account of the soccer training movie he had seen. Ruth criticized their table manners, asked me how long I was going to wallow at home, and then expressed horror when I told her I was going to work on Monday. Generally, she was her usual self, just a little worse, which was true of the rest of us too. She also served the best smothered pork chops ever made and her usual first-rate trimmings. She brightened up when the boys both asked for seconds and I praised her pork chops and the sweet potato soufflé for a solid minute.

After dinner, I cleared and the two of us washed and dried while the boys watched TV. I never knew how to talk to Ruth; my father-in-law was the easy one, and when Alfred died I lost my biggest fan. I looked over at Ruth, scrubbing neatly stacked pots with her pink rubber gloves, which matched her pink and white apron, which had nothing cute or whimsical about it. She hadn't raised Lionel to be a good husband; she'd raised him to be a warrior, a god, a genius surrounded by courtiers. But I married him anyway, when he was too old to be a warrior, too tired to be a god, and smart enough to know the limits of his talent.

I thought about life without my boys, and I gave Ruth a little hug as she was tugging off her gloves. She humphed and wiped her hands on her apron.

"You take care of yourself, now. Those boys need you more than ever." She walked into the living room and announced that it was time for us to go, since she had a church meeting.

We all thanked her, and I drove home with three pink Tupperware containers beside me, making the car smell like a pork chop.

I wanted to put Buster to bed, but it was only eight o'clock. I let him watch some sitcoms and changed out of my clothes into my bathrobe. Lion came into the hall in a fresh shirt.

"Going out?" He looked so pretty in his clean white shirt.

"Yeah, some of the guys want to go down to the Navigator. I said I'd stop by, see who's there. Don't wait up."

I was surprised but delighted. I tossed him the keys. "Okay, drive carefully."

Buster got himself into pajamas and even brushed his teeth without my nagging him. He had obviously figured out that I was not operating at full speed. I tucked him in, trying to give him enough hugs and kisses to help him get settled, not so many that he'd hang on my neck for an extra fifteen minutes. I went to sit in the kitchen, staring at the moths smacking themselves against the screen door. I could relate to that.

I read a few magazines, plucked my eyebrows, thought about plucking the gray hairs at my temples, and decided not to bother. Who'd look? Who'd mind, except me?

Finally, I got into bed, and got out about twenty minutes later. I poured myself some bourbon and tried to go to sleep again, thinking that I hadn't ever really appreciated what it took Lionel to get through life sober. I woke up at around four, anticipating Buster. But there, leaning against the doorway, was Lion.

"Ma." He sounded congested

"Are you all right?"

"Yeah. No. Can I come in?"

"Of course, come in. What is it, honey?"

He sat on the bed and plucked at my blanket, and I could smell the beer and the sweat coming off him. I sat up so we could talk, and he threw his arms around me like a drowning man. He was crying and gasping into my neck, and then he stopped and just rested his head against my shoulder. I kept on patting his back, rubbing the long muscles under the satiny skin. My hands were cold against his back.

Lion lifted his head and looked into my eyes, his own eyes like pools of coffee, shining in the moonlight. He put his hand up to my cheek, and then he kissed me and my brain stopped. I shut my eyes.

His kisses were sweet and slow; he pushed his tongue into my mouth just a little at a time, getting more confident every time. He began to rub my nipples through my nightgown, spreading the fingers on one big hand wide apart just as his father used to, and I pulled away, forcing my eyes open.

"No, Lion. You have to go back to your room now." But I was asking him, I wasn't telling him, and I knew he wouldn't move.

"No." And he put his soft plummy mouth on my breast, soaking the nightgown. "Please don't send me away." The right words.

I couldn't send my little boy away, so I wrapped my arms around him and pulled him to me, out of the darkness.

It had been a long time since I was in bed with a young man. Lionel was forty-two when I met him and, before that I'd been living with a sax player eight years older than I was. I hadn't made love to anyone this young since I was seventeen and too young myself to appreciate it.

His body was so smooth and supple, and the flesh clung to

the bone; when he was above me, he looked like an athlete working out; below me, he looked like an angel spread out for the world's adoration. His shoulders had clefts so deep I could lay a finger in each one, and each of his ribs stuck out just a little. He hadn't been eating enough at school. I couldn't move forward or backward, and so I shut my eyes again, so as not to see and not to have to think the same sad, tired thoughts.

He rose and fell between my hips and it reminded me of Buster's birth; heaving and sliding and then an explosive push. Lion apologized the way men do when they come too soon, and I hugged him and felt almost like myself, comforting him. I couldn't speak at all; I didn't know if I'd ever have a voice again.

He was whispering, "I love you, I love you, I love you." And I put my hand over his mouth until he became quiet. He tried to cradle me, pulling my head to his shoulder. I couldn't lie with him like that, so I wriggled away in the dark, my arms around my pillow. I heard him sigh, and then he laid his head on my back. He fell asleep in a minute.

I got up before either of them, made a few nice-neighbor phone calls, and got Buster a morning play date, lunch included, and a ride to soccer camp. He was up, dressed, fed, and over to the Bergs' before Lion opened his eyes.

Lion's boss called and said he was so sorry for our loss but could Lionel Junior please come to work this morning.

I put my hand on Lion's shoulder to wake him, and I could see the shock and the pleasure in his eyes. I told him he was late for work and laid his clothes out on his bed. He kept opening his mouth to say something, but I gave him toast and coffee and threw him my keys.

"You're late, Lion. We'll talk when you get home."

"I'm not sorry," he said, and I almost smiled. Good, I

47

thought, spend the day not being sorry, because sometime after that you're gonna feel like shit. I was already sorrier than I'd ever been in my whole life, sorry enough for this life and the next. Lion looked at me and then at the keys in his hand.

"I guess I'll go. Ma . . . Julia . . . "

I was suddenly, ridiculously angry at being called Julia. "Go, Lion."

He was out the door. I started breathing again, trying to figure out how to save us both. Obviously, I couldn't be trusted to take care of him, I'd have to send him away. I thought about sending Buster away too, but I didn't think I could. And maybe my insanity was limited to the Lion, maybe I could still act like a normal mother to Buster.

I called my friend Jeffrey in Falmouth and told him Lion needed a change of scene. He said Lion could start housepainting tomorrow and could stay with him since his kids were away. The whole time I was talking, I cradled the bottle of bourbon in my left arm, knowing that if I couldn't get through the phone call, or the afternoon, or the rest of my life, I had some help. I think I was so good at helping Lionel quit drinking because I didn't have the faintest idea why he, or anybody, drank. If I met him now, I'd be a better wife but not better for him. I packed Lion's suitcase and put it under his bed.

When I was a lifeguard at camp, they taught us how to save panicky swimmers. The swimmers don't realize that they have to let you save them, that their terror will drown you both, and so sometimes, they taught us, you have to knock the person out to bring him in to shore.

I practiced my speech in the mirror and on the porch and while making the beds. I thought if I said it clearly and quietly he would understand, and I could deliver him to Jeffrey, ready to start his summer over again. I went to the grocery store and bought weird, disconnected items: marinated artichoke hearts for Lionel, who was dead; red caviar to make into dip for his son, whose life I had just ruined; peanut butter with the grape jelly already striped into it for Buster, as a special treat that he would probably have outgrown by the time I got home; a pack of Kools for me, who stopped smoking fifteen years ago. I also bought a wood-refinishing kit, a jar of car wax, a six-pack of Michelob Light, five TV dinners, some hamburger but no buns, and a box of Pop-Tarts. Clearly the cart of a woman at the end of her rope.

Lion came home at three, and I could see him trying to figure out how to tackle me. He sat down at the kitchen table and frowned when I didn't say anything.

I sat down across from him, poured us each a glass of bourbon, and lit a cigarette, which startled him. All the props said "Important Moment."

"Let me say what I have to say and then you can tell me whatever you want to. Lion, I love you very much and I have felt blessed to be your mother and I have probably ruined that for both of us. Just sit there. What happened was not your fault, you were upset, you didn't know. . . . Nothing would have happened if I had been my regular self. But anyway . . . " This was going so badly I just wanted to finish my cigarette and take him to the train station, whether he understood or not. "I think you'd feel a lot better and clearer if you had some time away, so I talked to Jeffrey—"

"No. No, goddamnit, I am not leaving and I wasn't upset, it was what I wanted. You can't send me away, I'm not a kid anymore. You can leave me, but you can't make me leave." He was charging around the kitchen, bumping into the chairs, blind.

I just sat there. All of a sudden, he was finding his voice, the one I had always tried to nurture, to find a place for between his father's roar and his brother's contented hum. I was hearing his debut as a man, and now I had to keep him down and raise him up at the same time.

"How can it be so easy for you to send me away? Don't you love me at all?"

I jumped up, glad to have a reason to move. "Not love you? It's because I love you, because I want you to have a happy, normal life. I owe it to you and I owe it to your father."

He folded his arms. "You don't owe Pop anything. He had everything he wanted, he had everything." The words rained down like little blades.

I ignored what he said. "It can't be, honey. You can't stay."

"I could if you wanted me to."

He was right. Who would know? I could take my two boys to the movies, away for weekends, play tennis with my stepson. I would be the object of a little pity and some admiration. Who would know? Who would have such monstrous thoughts, except Ruth, and she would never allow them to surface. I saw us together and saw it unfolding, leaves of shame and pity and anger, neither of us getting what we wanted. I wanted to hug him, console him for his loss.

"No, Lion."

I reached across the table but he shrugged me off, grabbing my keys and heading out the door.

I sat for a long time, sipping, watching the sunlight move around the kitchen. When it was almost five, I took the keys from Lionel's side of the dresser and drove his van to soccer camp. Buster felt like being quiet, so we just held hands and listened to the radio. I offered to take him to Burger King, figuring that the automated monkeys and video games would be a good substitute for a fully present and competent mother. He was happy, and we killed an hour and a half there. Three hours to bedtime.

We watched some TV, sitting on the couch, his feet in my lap. Every few minutes, I'd look at the clock on the mantel and then promise myself I wouldn't look until the next commercial. Every time I started to move, I'd get tears in my eyes, so I concentrated on sitting very still, waiting for time to pass. Finally, I got Buster through his nightly routine and into bed, kissing his cupcake face, fluffing his Dr. J pillow.

"Where's Lion? He said he'd kiss me good night."

"Honey, he's out. He'll come in and kiss you while you're sleeping."

"Where is he?"

I dug my nails into my palms; with Buster, this could go on for half an hour. "He's out with some friends, Bus. I promise he'll kiss you in your sleep."

"Okay. I'm glad he's home, Mama."

How had I managed to do so much harm so fast? "I know. Go to sleep, Gabriel Tyner Sampson."

"G'night, Mama. Say my full name again."

"Gabriel Tyner Sampson, beautiful name for a beautiful boy. Night."

And I thought about the morning we named him, holding him in the delivery room, his boneless brown body covered with white goop and clots of blood, and Lionel tearing off his green mask to kiss me and then to kiss the baby, rubbing his face all over Gabriel's little body.

I got into my kimono and sat in the rocking chair, waiting for Lion. I watched the guests on the talk shows, none of whom seemed like people I'd want to know. After a while, I turned off the sound but kept the picture on for company. I watered my plants, then realized I had just done it yesterday and watched as the water cascaded out of the pots onto the wood floor, drops bouncing onto the wall, streaking the white paint. I thought about giving away the plants, or maybe moving somewhere where people didn't keep plants. Around here, it's like a law. The mopping up took me about eight minutes, and I tried to think of something else to do. I looked for a dish to break.

Stupid, inconsiderate boy. Around now, his father would have been pacing, threatening to beat him senseless when he walked in, and I would have been calming him down, trying to get him to come to bed.

At about three, when I was thinking of calling the hospital, I heard my car coming up the street slowly. I looked out the kitchen window and saw him pull into the drive, minus the right front fender.

He came inside quietly, pale gray around his mouth and eyes. There was blood on his shirt, but he was walking okay. I grabbed him by the shoulders and he winced and I dug my hands into him in the dark of the hallway.

"What is wrong with you? I don't have enough to contend with? Do you know it's three o'clock in the morning? There were no phones where you were, or what? It was too inconvenient to call home, to tell me you weren't lying dead somewhere? Am I talking to myself, goddamnit?"

I was shaking him hard, wanting him to talk back so I could slap his face, and he was crying, turning his face away from me. I pulled him into the light of the kitchen and saw the purple bruise, the shiny puff of skin above his right eyebrow. There was a cut in his upper lip, making it lift and twist like a harelip.

"What the hell happened to you?"

"I got into a little fight at the Navigator and then I had sort of an accident, nothing serious. I just hit a little tree and bumped my head."

"You are an asshole."

"I know, Ma. I'm sorry, I'll pay you back for the car so your insurance won't go up. I'm really sorry."

I put my hands in my pockets and waited for my adrenaline to subside.

I steered him into the bathroom and sat him down on the toilet while I got some ice cubes and wrapped them in a dish towel; that year I was always making compresses for Buster's skinned knees, busted lips, black eyes. Lion sat there holding the ice to his forehead. The lip was too far gone.

I wasn't angry anymore and I said so. He smiled lopsidedly and leaned against me for a second. I moved away and told him to wash up.

"All right, I'll be out in a minute."

"Take your time."

I sat on the couch, thinking about his going away and whether or not Jeffrey would be good company for him. Lion came out of the bathroom without his bloody shirt, the dish towel in his hand. He stood in the middle of the room, like he didn't know where to sit, and then he eased down onto the couch, tossing the towel from hand to hand.

"Don't send me away. I don't want to go away from you and Grandma and Buster. I just can't leave home this summer. Please, Ma, it won't—what happened won't happen again. Please let me stay home." He kept looking at his hands, smoothing the towel over his knees and then balling it up.

How could I do that to him?

"All right, let's not talk about it anymore tonight."

He put his head back on the couch and sighed, sliding over

so his cheek was on my shoulder. I patted his good cheek and went to sit in the brown chair.

I started to say more, to explain to him how it was going to be, but then I thought I shouldn't. I would tell him that we were looking at wreckage and he would not want to know.

I said good night and went to my bedroom. He was still on the couch in the morning.

We tried for a few weeks, but toward the end of the summer Lion got so obnoxious I could barely speak to him. Ruth kept an uncertain peace for the first two weeks and then blew up at him. "Where have your manners gone, young man? After all she did for you, this is the thanks she gets? And Julia, when did you get so mush-mouthed that you can't tell him to behave himself?" Lion and I looked at our plates, and Ruth stared at us, puzzled and cross. I came home from work on a Friday and found a note on the kitchen table: "Friends called with a housepainting job in Nantucket. Will call before I go to Paris. Will still do junior year abroad, if that's okay. L." "If that's okay" meant that he wanted me to foot the bill, and I did. I would have done more if I had known how.

It's almost summer again. Buster and I do pretty well, and we have dinner every Sunday with Ruth, and more often than not, we drive her over to bingo on Thursday evenings and play a few games ourselves. I see my husband everywhere; in the deft hands of the man handing out the bingo cards, in the black olive eyes of the boy sitting next to me on the bench, in the thick, curved back of the man moving my new piano. I am starting to play again and I'm teaching Buster.

Most nights, after I have gone to bed, I find myself in the living room or standing on the porch in the cold night air. I tell myself that I am not waiting, it's just that I'm not yet awake.

Three Stories

Hyacinths

The Sight of You

Silver Water

Hyacinths

My father was not a careless man. He had taken measure of the world's violence and his own, and he was sometimes ashamed and sometimes frightened, but he was not careless.

He got up at four every morning, he wiped and shelved his tools every night, and every May twenty-two white hyacinths came up at the foot of the front steps. I pictured my mother planting the hyacinths, with much the same care, and a great deal more joy, than my father ever showed to me. I imagined her, with the help of the two brown portraits in the living room, as even-tempered and affectionate, with none of my father's dark turns or distance. Why a woman like that would marry a miserable soul like my father, I could not imagine. My aunts and uncles who had known her were as honest as people of that time and place could let themselves be; they did not say that she was a homely shrew (as everyone but me must have seen from the frowning photographs), but they did not tell me stories of her warmth and charm. My aunt Ida said that my mother loved me and did her best by me, and for that show of kindness to me and to my mother, I loved my aunt Ida more than the other aunts, even more than Aunt Myrtle, who sewed bear-shaped cushions for my bed, even more than Aunt Ruth, who gave me candied violets after the obligatory Sunday dinner to which she occasionally, properly, invited her sister's widower and her little nephew, me.

Each of my parents had one brother. My father had two sisters, Ida and Myrtle. My mother had Ruth. Her family was slight and dark, Jews who had come to Toronto in 1922 and made the mistake of continuing west. My mother was the county schoolteacher, an old maid by local standards and a Jewess, of whom there were very few in Manitoba at the time, believe me, but she seemed healthy and was single, and my Presbyterian father was already thirty-six and struggling to keep his farm alive. I imagine now that I can remember the orphaned look in his eye, that belligerent mistrust which barely conceals despair. I see it in many of my patients, I assume that they can see it in me, if they wish to look that closely.

Aunt Myrtle, my father's younger sister, lived in Winkler, a few miles from my parents' place in Rosebank. She and Uncle William ran the general store there and lived in the back with their two boys, Willie and Percy. She made our kitchen curtains, as well as the stuffed-bear cushions. I have no true memories of their faces, just the dusty lemon scent of the cushions and a pair of short red hands that also smelled of lemon verbena. My father and his brother, Francis, had fallen out as young men, and apparently both sisters sided with my father. Aunt Ida, older than my father by fifteen years, kept house for us, and my father treated her the way he treated his old hunting dog: obliged to be kind, after years of her willing service; resentful of being obliged, by his own rules, to give what he couldn't spare. We were both frightened of him, Ida and I, and at six and sixty, we could not conceal our infuriating uselessness. We would hide together in the henhouse, dawdling over the warm eggs and the scattering of cracked corn, until we thought we heard the stable door bang open and closed and could see him heading toward the fields, reins in one hand, canteen in the other.

Aunt Ruth, my mother's sister, had come to Rosebank to keep my mother company (or was herself desperate for companionship, I have no idea) and had married a tailor, the only other Jew for a hundred miles, I'm sure. As all the women in Rosebank did their own sewing, Uncle Morris repaired the leather and canvas goods the farmers wore out. They kept kosher as best they could, and one of my few memories of their home is watching him kill and kasher a chicken for Shabbat dinner. For Sunday dinner, we had the roast my father contributed and bowls of potatoes.

Uncle Hi (for Hiram, changed from Hyman) was my mother's successful doctor brother. When I was six, he and Aunt Fritzi (for Frieda—the social position she upheld in Duluth did not require her to further anglicize her name) invited themselves for a visit, as they had done for each of the three years since my mother's death.

In May, a pink envelope came, with only my name neatly written in large purple letters above our address in smaller print. Aunt Fritzi took no chances. Aunt Ida held the envelope up for me to admire and read the letter aloud, ignoring all of Fritzi's indicated inflection.

Darling David,

　　Your Aunt Fritzi and your Uncle Hi (who gave you the big blue truck last year, do you remember?) would like to come visit you this summer. When we come, we will celebrate your SIXTH birthday. What a big boy! We would like to come June 27 and 28, when Uncle Hi can get away from his practice. Please ask your father if this is all right. If we don't hear otherwise, we will be there June 27, with your birthday present and lots of birthday goodies.

　　We can't wait to see you, darling. Hugs and kisses from us to you.

At the bottom, in a curling purple scrawl, was Aunt Fritzi's name and the imprint of two fuchsia lips. Yes, I remembered their gift, since I had only the truck and my bear cushions to play with. And although I had no idea what "birthday goodies" could possibly include, there would be lots of them. I looked at the budding trees and longed for summer. Ida put the envelope in her apron pocket and looked out at the trees with me. She said, "Tell him after supper, when he's lighting his pipe." Since Ida, I have had no one in my life so simply decent. Perhaps people like that all died out in the middle of this century, to be replaced by the clever, the quick, and the entitled.

My father was not happy that Hi and Fritzi were coming, but he would not lower himself by saying no. Nor would he make himself ridiculous by asking Myrtle the favor of her telephone just to fend off visitors, visitors who were undeniably family of some kind. They would fill the house with Hi's cigar and Fritzi's geranium face powder, and each supper would be a tennis match of Hi and Fritzi's long, lobbing questions and my father's one-word answers, played so close to the net that the final sound barely escaped before he closed his lips.

My real birthday came and went as it probably had before: an angelfood cake baked by Aunt Ida and a long walk down to the barn with my father. He showed me the newest calf.

"Son, you're six now. You name that little calf and you take care of him. Whatever we get for him, half of it's yours." He put his hand on the back of my neck, and I could see his big brown fingers out of the corner of my eye. "Happy birthday."

Over the cake, for which Ida took out, and my father put back, the fancy gold-rimmed plates, they asked me for the calf's name, and I finally said Blackie, to please them. I think they were surprised, perhaps a little disappointed; they had labeled me "fanciful" in response to my night terrors and absentmindedness, and I could come up with only the dullest and most sensible of names. I didn't care for the calf, green grass slime dripping from its mouth, manure sticking to its black and pink rear, right at eye level for me. I had loved and named all nine barn cats, whom my father alternately ignored and damned, and had connived with Ida to save at least a dozen kittens from his hand.

They came. Aunt Fritzi stepped out of a big blue Roadmaster, carrying a shiny red-handled paper sack from Warner's, the nicest department store in Duluth. I took in the magnificent car, the smiles and nice smells of my aunt and uncle, and the rest of the world faded away as Aunt Fritzi began, in defiance of my father, to hand me present upon present. I hopped madly from one foot to the other, transported by greed.

I don't know what the grown-ups did while I opened my gifts. Five boxes, all wrapped, all with ribbon. I remember Ida and Fritzi watching, smiling at me and even at each other, and the sounds of Hi and my father in the background, remarkably similar rumblings, although Hi's voice rose and fell and my father's was as flat as the pine floor. At the end of supper, for which Ida served a roast even though it was only Saturday, my father announced that he had invited Ruth and Morris and

Myrtle and William and the boys to come by for a visit early Sunday afternoon.

"That's lovely of you, Walter. Really lovely." Aunt Fritzi, born without malice or sensitivity, put her hand over my father's, and Ida and I both watched his efforts to move his hand without acknowledging her touch. Uncle Hi offered my father a cigar, Ida went in to do the dishes, and the men sat on the porch, cigar and pipe burning, while Aunt Fritzi showed me how to play Pickup Stix until bedtime.

Fritzi and Ida got ready for the party as though it were their house and my father and uncle were early-arriving guests. I was scrubbed from ear to toe and back and put into navy shorts and a navy-and-white shirt. Fritzi had also bought a sailor's white beret, but I balked and Hi backed me up. Fritzi and Ida came downstairs, both smelling of Fritzi's perfume, Ida's chest and neck blotched red with excitement, or embarrassment, or even suppressed rage, for all I know. They were smiling, and Hi said something to Ida that made her smile more, her hand covering her mouth. Fritzi straightened Hi's tie and patted him on both cheeks. No one touched my father or commented on his appearance, and I cannot remember what he wore. I heard the rattle of Uncle Mo's car (women did not *have* cars) and stood on the porch, watching. All the grown-ups came out too, and Fritzi waved as the rest of us stood there, pleased to see them. Hi hugged his sister and brother-in-law, and Fritzi added kisses and little squeezes to her hugs. Aunt Ruth and Uncle Mo, who had been living in Branden for several years by then, nodded to my father and Ida and went back to the car for packages. Ruth had brought two pies, and a rock candy stick for me. Just as we got settled, Aunt Myrtle and Uncle William drove up with little Willie, who was bigger than me, and Percy, who was still just a baby and was allowed to stagger around the house in his diapers, toast crumbs all over his face.

The women began supper preparation in earnest, and I still remember Fritzi's pleated yellow dress rippling above and below one of Ida's flour-sack aprons. I stood on the porch with Willie and Percy; the grown-ups would not speak to us or bother to look for us until suppertime, and we went down to the barn. I knew Willie would be impressed by the calf since he had no barn and no animals, although he did have access to jawbreakers, red-hots, and whole packages of chewing gum. Percy trailed along behind us, moaning a little with excitement and exertion.

Willie liked the calf a lot more than I did and scratched it behind its ears and laughed when its filthy tail whipped past his face.

"It's my birthday present," I said, the calf's value increasing by the minute.

"Gee," he said, and Percy sat down on a bale of hay, repeating "gee" over and over.

"Let's look at this stuff," Willie said, remembering that he was the oldest cousin. He ran his hands over my father's tools and played at cutting off my hair with a pair of secateurs.

"You're not supposed to touch the tools," I said.

"No one's here." Pretending not even to look at me, he reached for a harness and dropped it over his head and shoulders.

We played cowboy for a while, taking turns as the whip-wielding rider and the wild stallion, and when we got tired of the harness, Willie hung it back up, which I found reassuring. In the far corner of the barn was an old china cupboard where my father stored his guns. Willie opened it, and we all stared at the rifles, which were unlike the other tools in the barn. They gleamed, long polished snouts and shiny stocks.

Willie picked one up and I told him to put it down, and as the butt came toward me and we slipped on the mud and hay, my ears burst and Willie's chest flew out behind him, terribly dark. I couldn't hear a thing, not even Percy crying, although I could see him and see far into his wide-open mouth; I could see his tonsils as he screamed. Willie lay on the ground, and I lay down beside him. I could hear again when the men came running in, first my father, my uncles behind him in city shoes. I pretended I was dead too, as I assumed I soon would be. My father lifted me up with one hand and began to hit me with the other. William must have been holding his dead son, he never touched me. When the aunts came, there was more screaming, and while Hi and Fritzi held my father's arm, Ida grabbed me and ran into the house, her breasts lying over my face. I saw Myrtle cover Percy's eyes with her apron as she carried him to the car. I never saw either of them again, and I remember the back of her dress, crisscrossed by muslin apron strings, and Percy's fat, bare, dangling legs.

I don't remember anything else until late that night. I was in bed, in my pajamas, and I was comfortable; someone, Ida or Fritzi or both, had taken care of me. My father came into my room with a candle and sat in the corner chair, leaving the door open.

I knew better than to defend myself. Excuses and claims of persecution only made him hit me harder; he could not abide cowards. I was too surprised by the fact that he was sitting in my room to pretend to be asleep.

"Well, David," he said, a rifle balanced on his knees. "People can't live like this, son. Not when their hands are unclean. Our hands are not clean, are they? Answer me."

"No, sir. Our hands are not clean." I tried to see my hands in the dark. I thought they were probably pretty clean, that whoever had put me in pajamas seemed to have scrubbed me up pretty thoroughly.

"Good boy." He raised his voice and looked down through the rifle sight. "'If thy right hand offend thee, cut it off.' This will be over in a minute. Over," he shouted as I pulled the covers up around my head. I heard Uncle Hi through the blankets.

"Okay, Walter. Okay."

"Get out, Hiram. Get the hell out."

Fritzi ran in and yanked me out of bed, taking the blankets with her. She carried me down the stairs and we sat at the bottom, listening to an argument I can no longer recall in detail. Uncle Hi came down and put his hand on my head. Ida kissed me and cried over me as they bundled me into the backseat, and I was astonished by her tears.

"Be a good boy," she said. "No fussing, no dwelling on the past. Be a good, good boy."

My father stood in the front yard, his pipe making a small light. Perhaps he thought I was asleep, or perhaps they had all agreed that it would be better just to whisk me away, or perhaps if he had gotten any closer he would have tried again.

They must have driven straight through, for I awoke in a yellow bedroom filled with bright hatboxes and domestic flourishes of every kind. Having never seen much decoration, I was dazzled by the curtains, roses *and* ruffles, and the sateen bedspread with yards more ruffles and a slick nylon surface unlike any I'd encountered. Fritzi brought me toast with no crusts and cocoa. I did my best to indicate that I was in excellent spirits, would be a good, good boy and no trouble at all, and could be depended upon not to dwell on the past.

The days were orgies of shopping, which I found a little boring and physically disturbing; I had rarely been touched and was unnerved by the pats and probing and friendly pinches of these high-heeled women and wet-haired men. But every expedition for a suit or a cute pair of tennis shoes was matched with a trip to the soda fountain or the toy store, or even to Warner's, where we bought blue truck curtains, a blue corduroy spread, and a rug shaped like a fire engine. As a consequence of killing my cousin Willie, I lived in splendor with parents far more adoring and agreeable than those I had originally been dealt.

Sometimes, at night, I broke a toy and pressed myself hard upon the sharp pieces, or lay on top of my bedspread until my hands and feet went numb with cold. I was afraid that my father had been right and that the loving impulse that had led him to arrange for Fritzi and Hi to rescue me (which was how I now understood our flight to Duluth) was really a weak-minded avoidance of the inevitable. Sooner or later, someone was going to blow out my chest, and perhaps it would be better to get it over with than to sit up in the dark, waiting for Willie.

My bedtime, and therefore my nightmare, was regularly delayed by arguments between my aunt and uncle.

"He's a Jew, Fritz. He has to be circumcised. Only in that miserable anti-Semitic wasteland would a Jewish boy not be circumcised."

"So he wasn't, so who cares? Let him *not* be a Jew. Let him be David Dunmore, our Presbyterian nephew."

"How can you, of all people, be ashamed?"

"Ashamed? I'm not ashamed, I'm realistic. What does he

need to be a Jew for? So he can become head of cardiology but never head of the hospital? What a choice. Why not let him lead a goyish life?"

"Because he's a Jew," Hi said, gentle but relentless.

After a week of this, I knew that my aunt Fritzi couldn't have babies because of terrible things that had happened to her when she was a girl, over there, and that she loved me more than life itself. I found out that Uncle Hi was very angry that he couldn't golf with some of the other doctors, except when they invited him, but that he was proud to be a Jew and that as his adopted son, as David Silverstein, I would make him prouder still.

Fritzi kept arguing, determined to spare me the life of a Jew and the surgery, which she described in bloody, beckoning images. They fought, more pained than angry, all summer. In the middle of August, with the nights becoming familiar and cool, I received a letter from my father. It was left at my place at the breakfast table, opened but without comment, as though it had sailed right from the mailman's pouch to my plate.

Dear David,

Be a good boy and be grateful. You can come home now. If they cannot bring you, I will come for you.

Your father,
Walter Dunmore

"I want to be a Jew," I said, even before I put down the letter. I thought tenderly and briefly of Ida, her heavy arms outstretched to me, and I thought of my cats. I thought that Aunt Fritzi might get me a kitten, and I made up my mind.

"Whatever you have to cut off, I want to be a Jew. I want to be a doctor like Uncle Hi."

Hi was determined to do it right. He called in the rabbi to explain everything to me, he told me stories of King David and Moses, and he told me how brave I was. I think I would have been less brave if I had understood what was going to happen to me. As it was, I had figured out that there would be a token mark made on my penis, which would hurt for a few days. I was ready.

Two doctors, the rabbi, who called me Dah-veed, and a full minyan made up of my uncle's friends and colleagues, waited for me in the operating room. They stood over me, their big hands tugging at the green masks pulled taut over their big noses, smoothing the green cloth under their black-framed glasses. Beneath the huge bright light, their eyes were invisible to me. Only their green faces and their uniformly clean hands appeared, each finger outlined in white light. I heard the kind voice of Dr. Riskind, who had come for dinner earlier in the week and had given me his gold cigar band. I heard his voice murmuring gently behind me, and then he strapped each of my arms down while someone else strapped my legs. I felt myself peeing, unstoppably, without wetness. They put a hard plastic mask over my face and told me to breathe in and count backward from ten. I sucked in bitter, dry air until my chest ached, and my head slowly pulled away from my body until they were miles apart. I woke up screaming with pain and then stopped. I am delivered, I thought, as tears ran down my face and blood darkened my lap.

Rose's Barbie doll tumbled between my legs, spiky feet first, and I handed it back to her, meeting her eyes in the rearview mirror. She giggled.

"Careful," my wife warned her. "One more toss and it's ours."

I had planned our usual August vacation by March, but late in May I suggested we take a short trip to Canada. I wanted my children to see Rosebank; I wanted to see it again, but only with them. My wife shook her head, in what I took to be amused disbelief, and said it was all right with her if it was a trip I really wanted to make.

"Don't you ever think of going back to Kansas?"

Galen is not given to smiling, but she smiled at this. "Never."

"Not just for a little visit?"

"Not for thirty seconds."

Our girls were six and eight and willing travelers, as long as they could read and color and ignore the scenery. The backseat looked like a small but modern library, and since we were not going to the beach or a fancy hotel, our destination was of no interest to Rose and Violet. Although she never said so, I know Galen was as astonished as I was that we had such delightful and unexpected children, fey, gentle, apparently happy.

They slept easily in the backseat, Rose's head on Violet's bare legs, her white-blond hair swinging in front of her blank dreaming face, trickling across Violet's thighs.

Galen was quiet beside me, as she usually was. I am quiet myself, and do not mistake silence for tranquility or goodness. I do not say what I feel, and people often take that for shyness, even kindness. I put my hand on Galen's and pressed lightly. She didn't look at me, but she didn't move her hand away. My first wife, warm and efficient, would have called Triple-A to map our vacation and arranged for comfortable motels and side trips of historic interest. Very little, beyond music and the children, interested Galen, and nothing, as far as I could tell, frightened her. The day we left, she packed a small bag for herself, a larger one for the girls, and sat down on the fender with a magazine, waiting to drive or be driven.

The girls woke up abruptly, Rose alleging that Violet had kicked her in the mouth and then righteously biting the offending foot. Violet screamed and Galen closed her eyes.

"Could you manage the girls, please?"

She didn't open her eyes. "They're fine, David."

They were not fine, they were moving toward hysteria, but I knew that would not prompt Galen to intervene.

"Stop it," I said, frowning like a father while Rose and Violet watched me in the mirror and pinched each other, silently and ferociously. I pulled over and looked at the map, too tired to drive any farther, unwilling to enter Rosebank at night.

"We're coming into Canada. Gretna, Schoenwiese, Rosengart, Haskett, Blumenfeld, Osterwick, Hochfeld, Schanzenfeld, Winkler, and then up to Rosebank. Rosebank is where Daddy was born."

"I thought you were born in Duluth, where Grampa Hi and Nana lived," Rose said.

Violet was laughing to herself, repeating the names.

"That's quite a list," Galen said.

Schanzenfeld, Winkler, Rosebank. I could smell manure and silage and Fels Naptha, the only cleanser Aunt Ida had ever used, carving thick slices off the white bar and rubbing them into my father's collars. I pulled into the first motel we saw, a real motel, like the ones of my Northland youth, nine shabby cabins in a horseshoe shape around a rutted gravel drive and an oval aqua pool in the center. The girls emptied out their backpacks, looking for swimsuits, leaving a familiar trail of dirty white socks, coiled panties, and stale, damp jeans. Galen pulled out her suit without disturbing any other layers, leaving me to watch the black moths gathering on the overhead light.

Hyacinths

When I stepped outside, the pool had turned deep violet and the night air was so thick it hid the fence and the chaises. I could hear the girls better than I could see them, since most of the evening light was provided by two bug boxes electrocuting mosquitoes in short cobalt bursts.

Violet was screaming "No, no!," giggling and gulping water, and I could hear Rose's falsely maternal reassurances and her giddy laugh and their splashing. I came toward the fence, groping for the gate, seeing only shadowy heads and hands in the water.

I heard one of them yell, "Daddy," and was flattered that I had been called first, and then frightened.

"Daddy, I can't find Vi," Rose screamed.

"Where is she?" I couldn't even see Rose.

"The end farthest from you," she said, with extraordinary lucidity.

Without my shoes, without my glasses, I dove into the dark water looking for my daughter, thinking, "Too late, too late," and reached my arms in front of me, pushing the water aside. I was about to come up for air when Violet's hand hit me in the face, and I pulled us both up, one arm around her twisting waist. She suddenly stopped working against me, stretching her body out to protect me from her frantic, involuntary kicks. We sat on the hard concrete, Rose hovering over us as Violet vomited, water flowing from her mouth and nose and eyes. She sat in my lap, cold, wet, and dense under three towels, and I rocked her back and forth, telling her it was all right, Daddy was here, we'd go home tomorrow. I heard Galen's footsteps on the gravel and was furious that she had not been at the pool in the first place, and grateful and pleased to have her as my witness.

I held Violet close, wiping her nose with the towel end,

enjoying the feel of Rose's arms flung over my shoulders and Galen's light hand on my back. I looked up at the night, as clear as the Rosebank sky I remembered, and I could see Willie, as I often did. Alive and chestless, he leans up against a bale of hay, one grubby, fat hand resting on the shotgun muzzle. He is smiling, not impatient. I have been spared, a small animal at the hands of a violent but distractible boy. Lucky this time.

The Sight of You

It was ninety-seven degrees and I took my kids to the club for a swim. Everybody was there, including my lover, Henry, his wife, Marie, and their two boys, whose names I forget. My husband, David, stayed home to mow the lawn and read the *Times*.

Henry and I didn't really see each other that much during the two years we were lovers. We could have, I think. I'm a musician; I could have practiced a little less. Henry ran a construction company; he was his own boss. All of our time together was shaved off something bigger, slivered into pieces so thin you could look right at them and never even see. Those two winters I would look out my window at dawn and see his crew plowing driveways. They were like angels in the snow, their little white and yellow lights turning softly in the storm, right into my bedroom.

I was watching Henry from the clubhouse deck as he showed the youngest boy how to swim, his big arms carving runnels in the water, clearing a path for the littler arms to move in. I wore huge sunglasses so I could watch him. That was all I really wanted, just to watch Henry, forever. I grew up on the Plains and didn't know how I'd longed for the ocean until my foot felt the first wave's edge. And I hadn't known the wordless, leaping power of beauty until I saw Henry.

Marie walked past my chaise looking the other way, and I tried not to blame her for her bad manners and tight red face. Grief made her ugly, and I know that she was not always ugly.

I lay back, calculating whether I had time to talk to Henry while Marie was wherever she was. I thought so and dove in from the pool's edge, surfacing next to him. Under his little boy's splashing, he put his hand on my waist, watching for Marie, who seemed to have a sixth sense about us. She worried that we were having an affair and complained, obliquely, about my presence. She never saw anything between us. I could have kissed him on the mouth that day, in front of all the neighbors, and everything would have been different.

He stood close to me and smiled. We could both look down and see his erection, even in the cold water. Marie came zipping out of the snack area, a bag of chips in one hand and a racket in the other.

"Hank, we've got a court. Go dry off and I'll get your sneakers." Among the club set, she was a serious tennis player. She stood there, looking down on us, her hands on her hips. She didn't move until Henry headed for the wall. Then she smiled at me and walked toward the court.

I followed him to the wall, watching the small drops quiver down his back. I didn't know I was about to speak. "Henry, I don't think this is working. What about our time together?" We were both surprised. "If you still want me to leave him, I will."

I swam across the pool and went back to my chaise. Henry

was still standing in the water, looking dazed. He hoisted himself out, emerging smoothly like a big dark dolphin, all muscle and flex, no visible bones. He glanced at me and then headed for the court, his tennis shirt clinging to his wide wet back. I put my chin on the deck's redwood railing and watched them play.

I always felt powerful with Henry, powerful and grateful. That day, I felt like God Almighty, holding a crowd of tiny people in one huge hand. I had wanted to hold just Henry, but somehow another six had climbed aboard. David had given me the only home I'd ever had, but like the little mermaid in the fairy tale, I was prepared to cut my true self in two and walk in pain and artifice just to dance with Henry, dazzled by all that unfamiliar light.

I thought about the girls and hoped they'd be all right. The three of us had been a team, and that wouldn't have to change. David had been a good father, better than most I've seen; he played Scrabble with them, went to their concerts, picked them up from swim team when I was touring, hugged them every day, and knew how to braid their hair. I thought Henry would help out the way he did with his boys, and nothing would keep David from Rose and Violet. I used to think the girls were like my arms, I didn't need anyone's help growing them or taking care of them. When Rose was an infant, she would sleep through my practicing but wake up as soon as I started to vacuum. I stopped vacuuming. And Violet, my baby, used to help the ushers at my concerts, tripping over her Mary Janes and her lavender organdy skirt, but knowing where every seat in the hall was. I took them most everywhere I went; we all loved music and new places and hotel rooms. David usually stayed home; he's a psychiatrist and never likes to leave his patients for too long.

I didn't know what would happen when Henry finished playing tennis. We would have to talk on the phone, work out details. The girls would go to music camp for a month, and I could move then if David wanted the house. Or maybe he'd move out. The house didn't matter much to me as long as I had my piano and a bedroom for the girls. I have to force myself to sleep in a bed, even now.

When I got home, I sat down at the piano and stared at the keys, waiting for a wave of guilt or panic that would tell me to stop.

Henry loved me the way I was taught Indians loved Nature; I was everywhere for him, in the air, in the light, seeping right into his skin. It scared me a little, how much he loved me, handing over everything he had. He would kneel in front of me, big man, putting his hands around my waist as though to snap me in two, and he'd say, "There is nothing I wouldn't do for you." And I would rest my hands in his black curly hair.

"Nothing," he'd say again.

And I said, "I know," and he'd relax and lay me on the bed.

It was like nothing else in my life, that river of love that I could dip into and leave and return to once more and find it still flowing, undisturbed by my comings and goings. And when we made love, it was the same. He would wash over me and into me and he didn't need me to smile, or cry out, or move. I lay there, like the riverbed.

I was orphaned at sixteen, by two lonely, curdled people who had hoped to divorce without too much scandal when I finished high school. Instead, their car hit a tree. I was sent off to boarding school by a committee of relatives and came home to visit Mrs. Wallace (the one my father hoped to marry) and

Dr. Davidson (the one my mother had in the wings). I went on being their memorial tribute to thwarted love and bad planning until I turned eighteen. I escaped to Juilliard and didn't answer their letters. Being an orphan didn't bother me.

While I was at Juilliard, I met David. He was finishing his residency in psychiatry, and I was one of his guinea pigs. I was nineteen, he was twenty-nine. My faculty adviser had noticed that I never went away for holidays, never had family in the audience, never had trouble paying my tuition. I told her the highlights of my personal history, and she turned her face away and suggested that I "talk to someone" at the Washington Square Clinic. I thought it had something to do with piano playing, so I went.

It was April, and the big waiting room was still wintry. All the chairs were gray plastic. As I put my feet up on one of them, I saw two men talking on the far side of the room. My hearing is acute, and I eavesdropped.

"I'll take her," said the tall, chubby one.

"No," said the other one, David. "You're full up this week, and anyway, you couldn't handle your countertransference."

"My countertransference? Please. All right, you take her. Take her."

I was smiling when David invited me into his cubicle.

"You have a lovely smile," he said, and then he frowned.

"Thank you. Why are you frowning?"

"I'm not. . . . I'm Dr. Silverstein and you're . . . Galen Nichols?"

"Yes."

"Well." He arched his fingertips together the way they must have taught him in Practical Psychiatry. "What can I do for you?"

77

"I don't know," I said, and I didn't say anything else.

We had three sessions like that, and at the end of the third I got up and shook his hand.

"Thanks for your time," I said. I liked him, he acted just like me.

Two weeks later, he called and asked how I was doing. A few weeks after that, he invited me to go for coffee. I went, and we sat in the Big Apple Coffee Shoppe for two hours while he told me that he was married but just couldn't stop thinking about me. I thanked him for the coffee and went home and listened to my most recent performance tapes.

After two more coffee dates, he asked me to have dinner with him.

"I can't take a break for dinner these days, we're rehearsing. But if you want to get something for yourself and come listen, you're welcome to."

David sat at the back of the auditorium until 1:00 A.M., and he walked me home.

"You play so beautifully. May I please come in?"

"Sure."

By then, I had figured out that he wasn't really like me at all, but he was a gentle, sweet man, not like the cowboys at home. He touched me as if I were made of glass and gold dust. At about 3:00 A.M. he jumped out of bed and into his jeans, mumbling how sorry he was. I was too tired to walk him to the door, so I blew him a kiss and told him to take the extra key.

"I'll call you," he said.

"All right."

When he called, though, I couldn't see him because I'd gotten a grant to study in Paris for the rest of the summer. I gave him my address at the pension and told him to take care. Three weeks later, Madame Laverre whispered that I had a visitor waiting in the courtyard. There was David, unshaven, an enormous bouquet of flowers in his shaking hands. I was glad to see him.

He said that he'd asked his wife for a separation and that she'd agreed. I didn't want to talk about it. We found a couple of jars for the flowers and walked along the river. He took a room down the hall and stayed for ten days. I'd practice or go to class during the day, and he'd visit museums and read. At night, we'd eat in the café and then have sex in his room. I slept in my own room. We had a nice time, and when he was leaving I said I'd call him in September.

I remember how he smiled then. "You've never called me."

"I will."

"Okay, I'll be in my own place by then, and I'll list the new number with Information right away so you can get it." He was swinging my hand back and forth. "Coming to Paris was the best thing I could have done. I love you, you know."

"I'm glad you came," I said. "Don't miss your plane." And he stroked my hair and cried for a minute before he left.

When I got back I did call him, and we spent most of our evenings together. For a year he asked me to marry him and I ignored him. I thought I'd be dead by the time I was twenty-five, I couldn't see getting married. One morning David started banging his fists on my kitchen table and said, "You are killing me. All I want is to love you, and you won't let me."

I got dressed and left him sitting in the kitchen. I bought a white silk shirt to go with my white jeans and called him from Macy's to meet me for a blood test. Ten years later, we had two girls, quiet, like me, but friendly. David is a good person, and I knew that women would be lining up six-deep, with casseroles, the minute I left him.

I walked into the kitchen, still thinking about the nice, normal woman who would become David's next wife, and watched him carry a plate of chicken to the grill, balancing tongs and a fork and a bottle of barbecue sauce. He had sent the girls to get out of their wet suits, and while I chopped red peppers and hulled strawberries I kept my head down, wondering if it'd be better to leave a note. He watched me putter, and after he had washed and dried his hands carefully, he rested them on my shoulders for just a second. Then he went into the living room and put on Vivaldi while I set the table.

After dinner, we let the girls bike around the neighborhood and we washed the dishes together. David went to work on an article, and I sat in the bedroom, in the bent willow rocking chair that we bought when I was pregnant with Rose, and waited for the phone to ring.

"Hi, it's Hank DiMartino." We were always very careful, in case a spouse picked up simultaneously.

"Hi. David's in his study." The study didn't have a phone, so that he wouldn't be disturbed. "How'd the tennis game go?"

"Not bad, considering that I was out of my mind. You looked so beautiful today, and you've made me so happy. You did mean it? You'll leave?"

"Yes."

"I can't believe that I'm going to wake up every morning for the rest of my life and look at your face on the pillow next to mine. I want to marry you, as soon as we can."

I was picking dead leaves off the fig tree in our bedroom. "I'll be yours until the stars fall from the sky, Henry. I don't have any thoughts about marriage." I also had some doubts about sleeping in the same bed. David was used to my slipping onto the floor during the night.

"I want us to belong to each other."

"That doesn't make any sense. You belonged to Marie, and

you're ready to divorce her. I belonged to David, and before that, he belonged to Nina. It's really silly, the whole idea."

"Gae, honey, I want to be with you and I want it to be forever."

"I want to be with you too, Henry." And I did.

David came into the bedroom. He mouthed, "For me?" and I shook my head. He stood in the middle of the bedroom, looking at me, before he went back to his study.

"I have to go. David's wandering around. I'll drive by the construction site tomorrow. Columbine Lane, right?"

"Right. That'll be great. I love you, you."

"I know. See you tomorrow."

David came to bed a little earlier than usual, and he laid his hand on my breast. After a while, he put his hand on my thigh, his sign, and I shifted my legs to let him enter me. It wasn't as nice as cooking to the Vivaldi, but it was really all right. I awoke on the floor. David had put a quilt over me and tucked his sweater under my head.

I put the sweater on and practiced for about three hours after the girls went out to play and David went downtown to see patients. This was one of my favorite times, and I didn't want to cut it short. I practiced some performance pieces I was having trouble with and threw in a little jazz at the end. My fingers were getting stiffer as I got older. I showered and went to meet Henry, wearing a shapeless blue shift that he hated. I drove over to Columbine Lane, where he was building a house.

His crew was there, taking a coffee break. Most of the guys knew me, or my car, by sight. Henry and I counted on the fact that most people, especially men, don't like to get into other people's business. I came and went freely, undisguised. Usually, I'd just pull over onto the ridge near his trailer and sit in the car waiting. Henry would come out after a few minutes and scrunch down by the window to talk to me about our schedules and try to work his plans around mine. Once in a while, if we had a chunk of time during the day, we'd go to a hotel. I would have gone to a motel, or even to the park, but Henry felt we deserved better. I didn't think it had much to do with what we deserved.

He saw me right away and hopped down from the unfinished patio. I could watch him run toward me and never tire of the sight, his right leg slightly stiff at the knee from an old baseball injury, his muscles flowing beneath his clothes. I wanted that ease, that perfect unconsciousness, to transform me so that I would never again find myself in the middle of traffic, paralyzed by the risk and complexity of the next step.

Once, the summer before, I'd been watching him from the clubhouse as he did his laps. He felt my eyes on him and he got out of the water, face turned to me, and came up the stairs to the deck, dripping water through the building. No one else was around.

"I can't not come to you," he said. "I just don't have any choice about it." And he gathered up my hair into little bunches and pressed them against his wet face, like flowers. After Rose and Violet, I loved that kind of love the most.

It wasn't his wanting me that got to me. That was nice, but not so rare in my life. Men see something in me, or something missing, that they like. It's that he didn't fight the feeling; a lot of times men want you and then they get mad about wanting you, whether they have you or not. He had never been angry with me, or disappointed, or blamed me for what I couldn't do. And more than that, it was that he was so beautiful and that beauty belonged to me.

When he got to my car, I swung the door open and he knelt

in front of me. I put my hand on his arm, breaking our public display rules, which now seemed irrelevant. He smiled down at my hand, a sunny, white smile that was like nothing I'd ever seen in my mirror.

"Ready to take the plunge?" he asked.

"I'm ready to tell David, after the girls go to camp. I can move out then, or he'll move out, and we can get started."

"Started? Galen, we're a lot further along than 'getting started.' I really do want to marry you, and I want us to try and get custody of the boys."

Shit, I thought. First of all, Marie does a perfectly fine job with the boys, it's not like they need to be rescued, and second of all, I could just see myself spending the next five years of my life trying to win over the older one. Making hot dogs and burgers when I've trained my girls to eat French, Thai, Indian, and whatever's put in front of them; having to wear a robe when I take a shower; going to tennis matches every weekend; stepping over GoBots and pieces of GI Joe.

"Henry, let's wait and see. Let's give ourselves a chance to enjoy ourselves, just be together and see how it goes."

He got very dark and his brows drew down. I didn't know what else to say.

"I don't have much choice, do I? If you don't want to take what I want to give you, I can't make you. But I'm going to keep asking you, and one of these days you're going to say yes. It's meant to be, sweetheart." He was smiling again; he believed everything he was saying.

Like hell, I thought. I was touched, of course, but I could never answer the same question over and over. And I don't believe that anything's written for us, certainly nothing good. I slept on the floor, I lost track of time, and love and death had always looked pretty much the same to me. David needed to marry someone crazy; Henry had mistaken me for someone *interesting*.

He put his big hand over mine, and I watched a little cloud of plaster dust settle on us.

"I have to go. I'll talk to you tomorrow." I slammed the car door and drove off, watching him shrink in the rearview mirror.

My arms and legs were cold, driving home through the woods, and I thought about what I was going home to. I pulled the car off the road, picturing Henry and his boys, and his kids with my kids, and Marie bitching about money, and Henry sitting in a studio apartment with mismatched plates, waiting for me to make his divorce meaningful, valuable, decent. Waiting for me to make his life beautiful. And when I'd finally get up to leave, he'd watch me go, letting me know that I was supposed to stay with him, that I was hurting him.

I got home about ten of twelve and called David between appointments. He picked up on the first ring.

"Dr. Silverstein here."

"Ms. Nichols here."

He sounded surprised and he laughed. I didn't call him often, since he was calling home once or twice a day at this point. I used to hate that when we were first married, and he finally stopped, but that year he had started again and I didn't say anything about it. He was right to be afraid.

"I could call Mrs. Stevenson for the girls and we could go to the Siam, just the two of us," I said.

"Okay, that would be fine. That would be nice."

I hadn't expected more than that. "Good. See you at home."

"Okay. I'm glad you called."

"See you at home."

84

"I love you," he said.

"I know. See you soon."

I practiced for another hour, and when the girls came in we took turns playing duets for a while, and then I had to go lie down. I fell asleep for about an hour, and when David woke me up I tried to focus and made the girls stir-fry vegetables and fried dumplings.

Our own dinner was pretty nice, smooth white platters of dark, peppery food, cold beer, and enough room for me to lie back against the cold vinyl seats. David kept reaching forward, touching my temples and my wrists, where my veins are big and blue.

"How do you keep so cool?" he asked. It was an old joke between us.

"No heart," I said.

He smiled, and I thought, I cannot do this again. I smiled back at him.

I drove down to see Henry the next day, and the guys waved to me. I got out of the car and went over to Henry and kissed him on the mouth, and then on both cheeks, and then at the corner of each perfect eye. He didn't smile.

"You're not going to leave him, are you? You're going to tell me that you can't do it, and I just don't want to hear it. Please, Galen, please, baby. Don't say it."

"I won't say I can't. That's too easy. I have to say that I'm choosing not to. I'm so sorry."

He looked me up and down for a minute, and he put his warm face into my neck. I could feel every bone in his face pressing in, but I stood fast.

"I had an offer for the business, a pretty good offer. I could go down to North Carolina, I could go back into business with my dad. Should I take it?"

"Do you want to?" I could see him going, striding loosely down a back road, the sun shining on him, wherever he was.

"No, goddamnit, I don't want to. I want to stay here and marry you and have a child with you, that's what I want. That's all I've wanted for two years, and if I can't have that, I don't even know what to want."

"I don't know what you should do. Does Marie want to move?"

"Of course. I haven't even told her about the offer. You know Marie, she'll have us packed before the ink's dry on the contract. Getting me away from you will make her very happy."

We smiled; Marie had been suspicious long before there had been anything between us, and somehow that had left us feeling slightly less guilty.

"I know." And I thought about having him near and him looking at me like he had a splinter in his heart and Marie looking at me the same way, only without the love.

"Take the offer," I said. "Move."

"Okay," he said, like a threat.

"Okay," I said, and I kissed him, just one quick time, and I closed my eyes until he walked away.

Silver Water

My sister's voice was like mountain water in a silver pitcher; the clear blue beauty of it cools you and lifts you up beyond your heat, beyond your body. After we went to see *La Traviata*, when she was fourteen and I was twelve, she elbowed me in the parking lot and said, "Check this out." And she opened her mouth unnaturally wide and her voice came out, so crystalline and bright that all the departing operagoers stood frozen by their cars, unable to take out their keys or open their doors until she had finished, and then they cheered like hell.

That's what I like to remember, and that's the story I told to all of her therapists. I wanted them to know her, to know that who they saw was not all there was to see. That before her constant tinkling of commercials and fast-food jingles there had been Puccini and Mozart and hymns so sweet and mighty you expected Jesus to come down off his cross and clap. That before there was a mountain of Thorazined fat, swaying down the halls in nylon maternity tops and sweatpants, there had been the prettiest girl in Arrandale Elementary School, the belle of Landmark Junior High. Maybe there were other pretty girls, but I didn't see them. To me, Rose, my beautiful blond defender, my guide to Tampax and my mother's moods, was perfect.

She had her first psychotic break when she was fifteen. She had been coming home moody and tearful, then quietly beaming, then she stopped coming home. She would go out into the woods behind our house and not come in until my mother went after her at dusk, and stepped gently into the briars and saplings and pulled her out, blank-faced, her pale blue sweater covered with crumbled leaves, her white jeans smeared with dirt. After three weeks of this, my mother, who is a musician and widely regarded as eccentric, said to my father, who is a psychiatrist and a kind, sad man, "She's going off."

"What is that, your professional opinion?" He picked up the newspaper and put it down again, sighing. "I'm sorry, I didn't mean to snap at you. I know something's bothering her. Have you talked to her?"

"What's there to say? David, she's going crazy. She doesn't need a heart-to-heart talk with Mom, she needs a hospital."

They went back and forth, and my father sat down with Rose for a few hours, and she sat there licking the hairs on her forearm, first one way, then the other. My mother stood in the hallway, dry-eyed and pale, watching the two of them. She had already packed, and when three of my father's friends dropped by to offer free consultations and recommendations, my mother and Rose's suitcase were already in the car. My mother hugged me and told me that they would be back that night, but not with Rose. She also said, divining my worst fear, "It won't happen to you, honey. Some people go crazy and some people never do. You never will." She smiled and stroked my hair. "Not even when you want to."

Rose was in hospitals, great and small, for the next ten years. She had lots of terrible therapists and a few good ones. One place had no pictures on the walls, no windows, and the patients all wore slippers with the hospital crest on them. My mother didn't even bother to go to Admissions. She turned Rose around and the two of them marched out, my father walking behind them, apologizing to his colleagues. My mother ignored the psychiatrists, the social workers, and the nurses, and played Handel and Bessie Smith for the patients on whatever was available. At some places, she had a Steinway donated by a grateful, or optimistic, family; at others, she banged out "Gimme a Pigfoot and a Bottle of Beer" on an old, scarred box that hadn't been tuned since there'd been English-speaking physicians on the grounds. My father talked in serious, appreciative tones to the administrators and unit chiefs and tried to be friendly with whoever was managing Rose's case. We all hated the family therapists.

The worst family therapist we ever had sat in a pale green room with us, visibly taking stock of my mother's ethereal beauty and her faded blue t-shirt and girl-sized jeans, my father's rumpled suit and stained tie, and my own unreadable seventeen-year-old fashion statement. Rose was beyond fashion that year, in one of her dancing teddybear smocks and extra-extra-large Celtics sweatpants. Mr. Walker read Rose's file in front of us and then watched in alarm as Rose began crooning, beautifully, and slowly massaging her breasts. My mother and I laughed, and even my father started to smile. This was Rose's usual opening salvo for new therapists.

Mr. Walker said, "I wonder why it is that everyone is so entertained by Rose behaving inappropriately."

Rose burped, and then we all laughed. This was the seventh family therapist we had seen, and none of them had lasted very long. Mr. Walker, unfortunately, was determined to do right by us.

"What do you think of Rose's behavior, Violet?" They did this sometimes. In their manual it must say, If you think the parents are too weird, try talking to the sister.

"I don't know. Maybe she's trying to get you to stop talking about her in the third person."

"Nicely put," my mother said.

"Indeed," my father said.

"Fuckin' A," Rose said.

"Well, this is something that the whole family agrees upon," Mr. Walker said, trying to act as if he understood or even liked us.

"That was not a successful intervention, Ferret Face." Rose tended to function better when she was angry. He did look like a blond ferret, and we all laughed again. Even my father, who tried to give these people a chance, out of some sense of collegiality, had given it up.

After fourteen minutes, Mr. Walker decided that our time was up and walked out, leaving us grinning at each other. Rose was still nuts, but at least we'd all had a little fun.

The day we met our best family therapist started out almost as badly. We scared off a resident and then scared off her supervisor, who sent us Dr. Thorne. Three hundred pounds of Texas chili, cornbread, and Lone Star beer, finished off with big black cowboy boots and a small string tie around the area of his neck.

"O frabjous day, it's Big Nut." Rose was in heaven and stopped massaging her breasts immediately.

"Hey, Little Nut." You have to understand how big a man would have to be to call my sister "little." He christened us all, right away. "And it's the good Doctor Nut, and Madame Hickory Nut, 'cause they are the hardest damn nuts to crack, and over here in the overalls and not much else is No One's Nut"—a name that summed up both my sanity and my loneliness. We all relaxed.

Dr. Thorne was good for us. Rose moved into a halfway house whose director loved Big Nut so much that she kept Rose even when Rose went through a period of having sex with everyone who passed her door. She was in a fever for a while, trying to still the voices by fucking her brains out.

Big Nut said, "Darlin', I can't. I cannot make love to every beautiful woman I meet, and furthermore, I can't do that and be your therapist too. It's a great shame, but I think you might be able to find a really nice guy, someone who treats you just as sweet and kind as I would if I were lucky enough to be your beau. I don't want you to settle for less." And she stopped propositioning the crack addicts and the alcoholics and the guys at the shelter. We loved Dr. Thorne.

My father went back to seeing rich neurotics and helped out one day a week at Dr. Thorne's Walk-In Clinic. My mother finished a recording of Mozart concerti and played at fund-raisers for Rose's halfway house. I went back to college and found a wonderful linebacker from Texas to sleep with. In the dark, I would make him call me "darlin'." Rose took her meds, lost about fifty pounds, and began singing at the A.M.E. Zion Church, down the street from the halfway house.

At first they didn't know what do to with this big blond lady, dressed funny and hovering wistfully in the doorway during their rehearsals, but she gave them a few bars of "Precious

Lord" and the choir director felt God's hand and saw that with the help of His sweet child Rose, the Prospect Street Choir was going all the way to the Gospel Olympics.

Amidst a sea of beige, umber, cinnamon, and espresso faces, there was Rose, bigger, blonder, and pinker than any two white women could be. And Rose and the choir's contralto, Addie Robicheaux, laid out their gold and silver voices and wove them together in strands as fine as silk, as strong as steel. And we wept as Rose and Addie, in their billowing garnet robes, swayed together, clasping hands until the last perfect note floated up to God, and then they smiled down at us.

Rose would still go off from time to time and the voices would tell her to do bad things, but Dr. Thorne or Addie or my mother could usually bring her back. After five good years, Big Nut died. Stuffing his face with a chili dog, sitting in his unair-conditioned office in the middle of July, he had one big, Texas-sized aneurysm and died.

Rose held on tight for seven days; she took her meds, went to choir practice, and rearranged her room about a hundred times. His funeral was like a Lourdes for the mentally ill. If you were psychotic, borderline, bad-off neurotic, or just very hard to get along with, you were there. People shaking so bad from years of heavy meds that they fell out of the pews. People holding hands, crying, moaning, talking to themselves. The crazy people and the not-so-crazy people were all huddled together, like puppies at the pound.

Rose stopped taking her meds, and the halfway house wouldn't keep her after she pitched another patient down the stairs. My father called the insurance company and found out that Rose's new, improved psychiatric coverage wouldn't begin for forty-five days. I put all of her stuff in a garbage bag, and we walked out of the halfway house, Rose winking at the poor drooling boy on the couch.

"This is going to be difficult—not all bad, but difficult—for the whole family, and I thought we should discuss everybody's expectations. I know I have some concerns." My father had convened a family meeting as soon as Rose finished putting each one of her thirty stuffed bears in its own special place.

"No meds," Rose said, her eyes lowered, her stubby fingers, those fingers that had braided my hair and painted tulips on my cheeks, pulling hard on the hem of her dirty smock.

My father looked in despair at my mother.

"Rosie, do you want to drive the new car?" my mother asked.

Rose's face lit up. "I'd love to drive that car. I'd drive to California, I'd go see the bears at the San Diego Zoo. I would take you, Violet, but you always hated the zoo. Remember how she cried at the Bronx Zoo when she found out that the animals didn't get to go home at closing?" Rose put her damp hand on mine and squeezed it sympathetically. "Poor Vi."

"If you take your medication, after a while you'll be able to drive the car. That's the deal. Meds, car." My mother sounded accommodating but unenthusiastic, careful not to heat up Rose's paranoia.

"You got yourself a deal, darlin'."

I was living about an hour away then, teaching English during the day, writing poetry at night. I went home every few days for dinner. I called every night.

My father said, quietly, "It's very hard. We're doing all right, I think. Rose has been walking in the mornings with your mother, and she watches a lot of TV. She won't go to the day hospital, and she won't go back to the choir. Her friend

Mrs. Robicheaux came by a couple of times. What a sweet woman. Rose wouldn't even talk to her. She just sat there, staring at the wall and humming. We're not doing all that well, actually, but I guess we're getting by. I'm sorry, sweetheart, I don't mean to depress you."

My mother said, emphatically, "We're doing fine. We've got our routine and we stick to it and we're fine. You don't need to come home so often, you know. Wait 'til Sunday, just come for the day. Lead your life, Vi. She's leading hers."

I stayed away all week, afraid to pick up my phone, grateful to my mother for her harsh calm and her reticence, the qualities that had enraged me throughout my childhood.

I came on Sunday, in the early afternoon, to help my father garden, something we had always enjoyed together. We weeded and staked tomatoes and killed aphids while my mother and Rose were down at the lake. I didn't even go into the house until four, when I needed a glass of water.

Someone had broken the piano bench into five neatly stacked pieces and placed them where the piano bench usually was.

"We were having such a nice time, I couldn't bear to bring it up," my father said, standing in the doorway, carefully keeping his gardening boots out of the kitchen.

"What did Mommy say?"

"She said, 'Better the bench than the piano.' And your sister lay down on the floor and just wept. Then your mother took her down to the lake. This can't go on, Vi. We have twenty-seven days left, your mother gets no sleep because Rose doesn't sleep, and if I could just pay twenty-seven thousand dollars to keep her in the hospital until the insurance takes over, I'd do it."

"All right. Do it. Pay the money and take her back to Hartley-Rees. It was the prettiest place, and she liked the art therapy there."

"I would if I could. The policy states that she must be symptom-free for at least forty-five days before her coverage begins. Symptom-free means no hospitalization."

"Jesus, Daddy, how could you get that kind of policy? She hasn't been symptom-free for forty-five minutes."

"It's the only one I could get for long-term psychiatric." He put his hand over his mouth, to block whatever he was about to say, and went back out to the garden. I couldn't see if he was crying.

He stayed outside and I stayed inside until Rose and my mother came home from the lake. Rose's soggy sweatpants were rolled up to her knees, and she had a bucketful of shells and seaweed, which my mother persuaded her to leave on the back porch. My mother kissed me lightly and told Rose to go up to her room and change out of her wet pants.

Rose's eyes grew very wide. "Never. I will never . . . " She knelt down and began banging her head on the kitchen floor with rhythmic intensity, throwing all her weight behind each attack. My mother put her arms around Rose's waist and tried to hold her back. Rose shook her off, not even looking around to see what was slowing her down. My mother lay up against the refrigerator.

"Violet, please . . . "

I threw myself onto the kitchen floor, becoming the spot that Rose was smacking her head against. She stopped a fraction of an inch short of my stomach.

"Oh, Vi, Mommy, I'm sorry. I'm sorry, don't hate me." She staggered to her feet and ran wailing to her room.

My mother got up and washed her face brusquely, rubbing it dry with a dishcloth. My father heard the wailing and came running in, slipping his long bare feet out of his rubber boots.

"Galen, Galen, let me see." He held her head and looked

95

closely for bruises on her pale, small face. "What happened?" My mother looked at me. "Violet, what happened? Where's Rose?"

"Rose got upset, and when she went running upstairs she pushed Mommy out of the way." I've only told three lies in my life, and that was my second.

"She must feel terrible, pushing you, of all people. It would have to be you, but I know she didn't want it to be." He made my mother a cup of tea, and all the love he had for her, despite her silent rages and her vague stares, came pouring through the teapot, warming her cup, filling her small, long-fingered hands. She rested her head against his hip, and I looked away.

"Let's make dinner, then I'll call her. Or you call her, David, maybe she'd rather see your face first."

Dinner was filled with all of our starts and stops and Rose's desperate efforts to control herself. She could barely eat and hummed the McDonald's theme song over and over again, pausing only to spill her juice down the front of her smock and begin weeping. My father looked at my mother and handed Rose his napkin. She dabbed at herself listlessly, but the tears stopped.

"I want to go to bed. I want to go to bed and be in my head. I want to go to bed and be in my bed and in my head and just wear red. For red is the color that my baby wore and once more, it's true, yes, it is, it's true. Please don't wear red tonight, oh, oh, please don't wear red tonight, for red is the color—"

"Okay, okay, Rose. It's okay. I'll go upstairs with you and you can get ready for bed. Then Mommy will come up and say good night too. It's okay, Rose." My father reached out his hand and Rose grasped it, and they walked out of the dining room together, his long arm around her middle.

My mother sat at the table for a moment, her face in her hands, and then she began clearing the plates. We cleared without talking, my mother humming Schubert's "Schlummerlied," a lullaby about the woods and the river calling to the child to go to sleep. She sang it to us every night when we were small.

My father came into the kitchen and signaled to my mother. They went upstairs and came back down together a few minutes later.

"She's asleep," they said, and we went to sit on the porch and listen to the crickets. I don't remember the rest of the evening, but I remember it as quietly sad, and I remember the rare sight of my parents holding hands, sitting on the picnic table, watching the sunset.

I woke up at three o'clock in the morning, feeling the cool night air through my sheet. I went down the hall for a blanket and looked into Rose's room, for no reason. She wasn't there. I put on my jeans and a sweater and went downstairs. I could feel her absence. I went outside and saw her wide, draggy footprints darkening the wet grass into the woods.

"Rosie," I called, too softly, not wanting to wake my parents, not wanting to startle Rose. "Rosie, it's me. Are you here? Are you all right?"

I almost fell over her. Huge and white in the moonlight, her flowered smock bleached in the light and shadow, her sweatpants now completely wet. Her head was flung back, her white, white neck exposed like a lost Greek column.

"Rosie, Rosie—" Her breathing was very slow, and her lips were not as pink as they usually were. Her eyelids fluttered.

"Closing time," she whispered. I believe that's what she said.

I sat with her, uncovering the bottle of Seconal by her hand, and watched the stars fade.

When the stars were invisible and the sun was warming the air, I went back to the house. My mother was standing on the porch, wrapped in a blanket, watching me. Every step I took overwhelmed me; I could picture my mother slapping me, shooting me for letting her favorite die.

"Warrior queens," she said, wrapping her thin strong arms around me. "I raised warrior queens." She kissed me fiercely and went into the woods by herself.

Later in the morning she woke my father, who could not go into the woods, and still later she called the police and the funeral parlor. She hung up the phone, lay down, and didn't get back out of bed until the day of the funeral. My father fed us both and called the people who needed to be called and picked out Rose's coffin by himself.

My mother played the piano and Addie sang her pure gold notes and I closed my eyes and saw my sister, fourteen years old, lion's mane thrown back and eyes tightly closed against the glare of the parking lot lights. That sweet sound held us tight, flowing around us, eddying through our hearts, rising, still rising.

Henry and Marie

Faultlines

Only You

Faultlines

Henry DiMartino said buying a lottery ticket gave you permission to dream of a better life. His wife, Marie, bought a lottery ticket every Friday morning on her way to work at the library. Henry never bought one. In order to dream of a new life, Henry contemplated having an affair with Mary Nordstrom, the lawyer for his construction company. Henry had had an affair five years ago, with a woman he wanted to marry, who didn't want to marry him. He had stood in his sons' bedrooms, looked at their beloved faces, and thought, "I can do this. I can leave you." It took two years for him to stop being ashamed that the only reason his children had a father to play ball with every night and to help them with their homework was that the woman he loved didn't love him back. When he realized he wouldn't die of heartbreak, but would live with some of it forever, he promised himself that the next time, if there was a next time, he wouldn't fall in love.

* * *

After five or six lunches, quick Chinese food across the street and pizzas in the office, Henry invited Mary and Nathan to dinner for the second Saturday in October. Marie started cooking Friday afternoon. Henry had designed their house, and the kitchen was the size of two full rooms, and the countertops were marble; it was his tribute to Marie's magnificent cooking. She made baby artichokes and gnocchi with basil and cream and veal alla marsala and a radicchio and orange salad. She made a peach tart with a hazelnut crust. Henry spent two hours choosing wines he thought Mary would like. He came upstairs, his arms full of wine bottles.

Marie waved to him silently as he put the wines in the dining room, and he waved back, excited and relieved. Marie was being so good about this, the whole evening looked different. They could all become friends, no harm would be done. He would go on flirting harmlessly with Mary, and he and Marie would go to St. Kitts in November and make love in a big room overlooking the warm blue water.

Marie tried to make her voice cheerful as she called out to Henry, "So, what's she like?" Marie knew that she was a terribly and unfashionably jealous woman, and she also knew, without admitting it, that her jealousy made Henry curl up inside himself, like a mollusk avoiding a pin. She could never decide, could never let herself know, if it was her jealousy that made her suspect he was having an affair when they lived in Connecticut, or if he really was. She didn't confront him because they moved away, and really because she could almost hear Henry admitting to the affair, could almost see him turning away from her, without apology. At night, as they got ready for bed, Marie would scowl, thinking that it was so unfair that they had both started out as attractive, athletic teenagers but Henry had matured into a startlingly handsome, broad-chested man with a permanent tan, white teeth, and black curly hair, made more beautiful by a few silver strands. Marie looked like a fairly trim, better-dressed version of her late mother. Henry didn't love her less for that, she knew. But his eyes didn't linger upon her when she undressed, and she knew that too, and he knew it and they both felt ashamed, and beyond that, obscurely resentful. Henry encouraged Marie to work out with him, but she always made it sound like a vain and childish thing for a grown-up to do. Henry did two hundred sit-ups and one hundred push-ups six days a week. Four days a week, he rode his exercycle for forty-five minutes.

Henry had no wish to tell Marie what Mary was like, but he couldn't resist talking about her, sliding his tongue over her name the way he dreamt of sliding it over the pulsing vein above her collarbone. Henry knew, having been married to Marie for twenty years, that the moment he described Mary the day would be ruined. And if he said nothing, the evening would be ruined, perhaps more dramatically, when Marie laid eyes on Mary. As Henry played with the wine bottles, he assessed his choices: ruin the day now and hope that by dinnertime Marie would have pulled herself together, or enjoy the rest of the afternoon, ignore the hot hole of his ulcer, and watch the evening collapse as Marie was helplessly rude to Mary and in a state of relentless hysteria until four in the morning. Henry poured himself a small glass of port and decided that a carefully crafted description of Mary would be better than just surprising Marie when Mary walked through the door. He went into the kitchen.

Marie braced herself for Henry's answer. Not a blonde, please.

"She's tall, kind of skinny, very short hair. She's smart, she did a great job with the contracts for that development in Laurel Springs. Her husband seems like a nice guy, he came by the office once. He's a writer, he writes about his family, Mary said, about growing up Jewish in North Carolina, which must have been a trip." Henry leaned against the counter, willing himself to look into Marie's eyes and smile, feeling the warmth of the port and of having said her name.

He could have said, "She is a pale, pale blonde, just like the other one. But Gae was soft and dreamy and made me want to wrap her up and carry her off to a better world. This one is cool and tough and loves baseball and runs twenty miles a week. When the light shines on that cap of blond hair and her pale blue eyes lie right on me like I am the only person in the room, I stop breathing because the tension in my chest is so great. And if I don't 'run into her,' I 'drop by,' and if that doesn't work I call and beg her to share a pizza with me, and as we sit there and drink beer from the same bottle I think about those long white legs wrapped around me, and she grins like she knows what I'm thinking and she doesn't mind. Also, something else you don't want to hear because you will feel about this exactly the way I do, Nathan isn't her husband. They've been living together for years, but you and I know that's not the same. And even though she says, other people say, it makes no difference, I hug that fact. She's not really his. And even though I don't love her, don't want to grow old together, if I don't have her I will never draw an easy breath again. That's what you really wanted to know. A blonde so pale she doesn't have to shave her legs."

Mary was Marie's nightmare, and Marie knew it and so did Henry. And so, in a way, did Mary, although she didn't want to know it and felt both flattered and guilty. Nathan would know it after the dinner party, since he was a good observer most of the time and not unused to men being attracted to

Mary. Nathan thought Mary was very good-looking, beautiful in her way, but he loved her for her brains and her humor and her easy competence. Henry thought she was flawlessly beautiful and would have traded away her humor and her competence for one night beside her. When Mary looked at Henry, the longing in his eyes moved her terribly, moved her away from Nathan, even though she knew that what Henry was longing for would be gone in another ten years.

Marie tried not to start screaming when she heard what Henry said, and what he didn't say. If he didn't mention hair color, the woman was obviously a blonde. She went to the stove and cooked, with skill and hatred. She would give that bitch and her castrato husband a meal they'd both remember; a peach tart that would melt on her lying tongue, gnocchi that would rest lightly in his gutless stomach, may they choke on it all and never find water.

Henry announced that he was going to take a look at the garden. Before he went outside, he slipped into the bedroom to think about what to wear for Mary. He knew he looked good in his suits, something Nathan, the writer, probably never wore. He couldn't very well wear his eight-hundred-dollar Italian suit for a casual dinner, Marie would tear it off his back. He wanted to look relaxed but not like some bricklayer, some greaseball tidied up for a special occasion. Henry wanted to lay out his clothes and fuss over them, but Marie would be listening for him to go out and garden. Mentally, he took out his black flannel slacks, a white shirt with a thin red stripe, and a red cashmere cardigan that Marie had bought for his fortieth birthday. He loved that sweater; the shape reminded him of his father and grandfather in the back of his grandfather's grocery store; the soft, monied material reminded him of how far he had come from sawdust and overripe vegetables.

He checked to see if his black lizard belt was in the drawer and looked for his black socks with the small gray pattern. Henry hurried out to rake leaves and to dream of Mary unbuttoning his shirt, her fingers pulling at his belt buckle. He enjoyed talking to her and admired her quick wit, but he never daydreamed of their conversations. He thought only of her square, dimpled chin, her powerful legs, her small white breasts and pointy nipples.

While she pulverized basil and sautéed pignoli, Marie also thought about what to wear. She couldn't wear white because she was bound to spatter something on it, and she wouldn't wear pants because as far as she was concerned she looked like a cow from the rear. She would not look bad in front of this woman. She would wear the heavy gold necklace Henry bought her in Florence for their twentieth anniversary, and she would add the diamond and gold earrings they picked out together in Bermuda. Let her look. She decided to wear a black and red blouse and a black pleated skirt. Marie always wore heels, even at home.

Mary was also thinking about what to wear, but she was able to talk about it with Nathan, who was bemused but willing.

"I don't know how formal they are. At work Henry's always in a suit, but I don't know." While she was talking, Mary was fingering a pale blue silk dress with short sleeves and no back. It showed off all her best features and created the illusion of a bust. She would have preferred darker eyelashes and a smaller ass, but she had been using mascara since she was twelve, and since the men in her life had always liked her ass, she had come to like it too. It was ridiculous to wear the silk dress; Nathan would think she was crazy. She took out high-waisted gray gabardine pants and a white silk blouse, and she put on dangling silver earrings that Nathan had given her a few birthdays ago, and a wide gray suede belt to emphasize her small waist.

"You look great," Nathan said, smiling. "Of course, if they're both in formal evening wear, we'll be a little embarrassed."

Mary smiled back; she loved Nathan and his fine, searching mind and his sweet humor and his endless patience. She could tell that Henry was smart enough but not brilliant, that he had a highly conventional sense of humor and an ugly, arrogant streak. She had told Nathan all those things about her new "office friend," but she didn't say:

"He is so hot for me he's smoking, and when he comes into my office, Alice, who wouldn't bring coffee to the Pope, falls all over herself to bring him coffee just the way he likes it. He is the sexiest thing I've ever seen, and I guess—I know—that I've just got to have him. Just once, Nathan, I swear, and then I'll be right back. You won't even notice I'm gone."

She smiled at Nathan and buffed her nails while he put on the gray corduroy pants and the black turtleneck he wore from now until April, at which time he switched to khakis, sandals, and a white cotton shirt.

Nathan and Mary found the house easily and congratulated each other, since neither of them had a sense of direction. Mary reached into the backseat for the house gift, a pot of white mums resting prettily in a black straw basket. She wanted to please Marie, and she wanted to show Henry what a nice person she was, and beyond that, she would never dream of going to a dinner party without a gift. And if Marie wasn't pleased or wasn't smart enough to pretend to be pleased, well, that would be her mistake.

There was enough bustle over the introductions and admiring of the house and exclaiming over the mums that the first eight minutes went smoothly and they all revised their opinions about how the evening would go. It was only when they all sat down in the living room and looked at each other that the mood began to swing downward.

"What lovely earrings," Mary said to Marie, and Marie touched her ears, proudly.

"Henry got them for me in Bermuda. I just love them."

Everyone smiled at Henry, and the two women talked about jewelry, which they both liked, although their tastes were rather different, and they talked about Italian leathers, about which they agreed, and then the four of them talked about Italy and the air pollution in Rome and about travel in general. Nathan told a few funny, self-deprecating stories about his backpacking days in Europe, when he didn't speak any foreign languages, and Marie smiled at him. While everyone beamed messages at him, Nathan tried to keep track of Marie's emphatic enthusiasm and Mary's affectionate appreciation and Henry's watchful smile.

All through dinner, Marie talked to Nathan and to Mary, and Mary focused on Marie, and the only one who talked to Henry was Nathan.

Red wine gave Mary migraines, and Marie never drank wine if she could help it, and the two men finished a bottle and a half of St. Amour, which Nathan praised, making Henry like him a little more. Henry missed having someone he could talk to about wine, someone to go in on a case with him. When Nathan said he fished, Henry found himself thinking that this was really quite a decent guy, not exactly a ball of fire, but a good guy and much more down-to-earth than he expected a writer to be. Henry thought maybe they could go out fishing together some Sunday morning.

Nathan thought Henry was a salt-of-the-earth type and certainly a very decent guy, even if he wasn't the brightest or most interesting person around. And that St. Amour was superb. Nathan hadn't had wine like that since he moved back from New York ten years ago. When Henry said he also liked to fish, Nathan wondered how it would be to fish with a companion.

The dinner conversation swirled around work briefly, which bored everyone, around Nathan's writing, which embarrassed him, around the DiMartino children, at Marie's insistence, and then around great Italian red wines, at which point both women raised their eyebrows and cleared the table, bringing them all back to a safe and mildly diverting conversation about kitchen appliances.

"Henry bought me a pasta machine last Mother's Day. I like it."

"Really? Can you use it for gnocchi?" Nathan liked talking about kitchen appliances; Mary had lived on yogurt and frozen dinners until she met Nathan.

"Yes, I just love it. It even comes with a ravioli press, and you hardly have to clean it. Everything goes into the dishwasher."

"You're kidding. I'll help you with the coffee and you can show me, before I rush out and buy one in an impulsive fit brought on by your marvelous cooking. Really, Marie, just fabulous."

Marie, charmed by Nathan's Southern manners and amazed to find a man who cooks, lets him lead her into the kitchen, almost forgetting that Mary and Henry will now be alone together.

As the kitchen door swings shut, Henry calls out, "All right, you guys get dessert and I'll show Mary the garden."

Mary smiles politely, not at all the impish, promising grin she has given Henry at their lunches; Marie is just too nice, and they have these great kids who now have names, Claude and Giulio, and even though Henry's still incredibly handsome, that doesn't mean she has to sleep with him. They can just be good friends and flirt a little bit, and since Nathan seems to like Henry and hasn't had a male friend for ages, the four of them will have dinner from time to time.

Mary follows Henry through the French doors onto the patio to look at the brilliant zinnias and amber mums and the soft, tenacious clematis, which has woven itself along the side of the house. He flicks on the patio lights and hands her a match for the squat citronella candles. As she is lighting them, Henry tells Mary how much he enjoys Nathan's storytelling. Mary praises Marie's cooking and says that it will be hard to keep up with her when Henry and Marie come to their house for dinner.

As they turn to go back to the house, one thin black heel catches on the edge of a flagstone, and Mary stumbles. He catches her and his right arm goes around her waist and the other behind her neck, and she lets her head fall back into the damp crook of his arm.

The flowers and the thick lemony air hum in their ears, drowning out the hiss of the espresso machine and the faint clinking of small cups into saucers.

A perfect kiss, like a perfect beach, or a perfect diamond, is not so common in our lives that it can be ignored. As Marie calls them for dessert, they loosen their arms but discover they cannot part, they are as inseparable as color and light.

Only You

Marie, who is not a very sexual person, who cannot forgive her body or its middle-aged alterations, gets almost all her needs met at The Cut Above, Alvin Myerson's beauty salon. When Alvin opened the shop, some friends told him to change his name to André or even to Alain. He couldn't be bothered and put his license, with ALVIN ROY MYERSON printed in large type, in the very front of the salon. "I traffic in illusion," he said, "not in lies." Marie, who cherishes her sons and loves and resents her husband, likes Alvin. She thinks they have something in common. All of Marie's women friends seem happy enough with their lives, those who aren't come over to Marie's house to make eyes at her handsome husband, who sometimes makes eyes back at them. Marie knows what attracts Henry, and it isn't women like her friends. They are all too maternal, too dark, too much like Marie for her to worry about.

Marie has gone in to discuss, for the third time, whether or not she should dye her gray-and-brown hair. She has been looking forward all day to feeling Alvin's strong hands on her shoulders as he pulls her head from side to side, describing the elegant, youthful woman she will become when he uses just a rinse to restore her natural color. Alvin makes it sound like she is only retrieving something that belongs to her, not doing something foolish and vain. Marie's fear of appearing vain, her conviction that she has nothing to be vain about, keeps her from making more than the slightest effort to look attractive.

"Come on," Alvin had said last week, bending down to whisper in her ear, "let yourself be beautiful."

"Henry's the beautiful one," she'd said, in a voice so hard and scared that the women sitting near her thought she must hate her husband.

When Joyce, the receptionist, tells Marie that Alvin is home today with the flu, Marie stares straight ahead at the racks of mousse and gel so that she won't cry; it's ridiculous to cry because your hairdresser isn't there, even if he is your good friend and you haven't seen him in a week. Marie drives much too fast to her father's bakery.

"Hiya, sweetheart. No work today?"

"I'm on a break, Pa. Let me have two of the baguettes, please."

"Sure, two baguettes. The boys like the white bread, you know. Hank likes the raisin pumpernickel. Having company? On a Wednesday?" Marie's mother died two years ago, and her father is in her house more than he is in his own.

"No. I've got a sick friend, so I'm bringing some bread and soup." Marie carefully skips pronouns. Her father wouldn't approve of her having a male friend, not even a hairdresser.

"Good girl, just like your mother, taking care of everyone. Hello, Mrs. Lottman."

Marie goes home to defrost a container of chicken and rice soup. She calls Alvin and tells him she'll be right over.

"I'm a mess, darling. Really. The place looks like shit and I look worse."

"Five minutes, Alvin, and don't get out of bed. The super can let me in." Marie grew up in Brooklyn and believes that all apartment dwellers are watched over by her uncle Sario or the local equivalent.

"Marie, there *is* no super. This is a condominium, and the manager, whom I have never, ever seen, lives on the far side of Chapel Hill. I'll let you in and then I'll crawl back into bed. God bless you."

Marie puts a few magazines and a quilt in the car while the soup microwaves, and writes a note for Henry saying she'll meet him at Claude's softball game.

Alvin looks just as bad as he said. His sandy brown hair is plastered to his skull, exposing his receding hairline, usually hidden by his bangs. At the shop he wears loose white wool pants and looks like the captain of the cricket team; lying in his king-sized bed, he looks like a dying John Barrymore, the face ravaged, the bones magnificent. Marie slices bread, reheats the soup, and gives the kitchen counters a quick wipe-down. She bustles, parodying her maternal self so that he won't be embarrassed. She cannot bear to embarrass him, she cannot bear for him to ask her to leave. She carries in the quilt and holds it up for his approval. Marie wants to tuck it in around him, to smooth it down the length of his torso.

"Gorgeous pattern. Rose of Sharon, right? You stole it from some old lady."

Since Alvin is trying to smile through a cold sweat, Marie pretends to be indignant. She puts the quilt over him, touching his damp cheek by accident.

Alvin takes both her hands in his and bends his head over them. "You have nice hands, Marie. Can I say something?"

"Sure. Say anything."

"No more of this coral shit on your nails, okay? You have small, pretty hands and pale olive skin. True reds and clear only, okay? And let's keep the nails oval, not pointed." He kisses the back of each hand and slides down beneath the quilt, which smells slightly, pleasantly, like the soup. "You're a doll," he says, closing his eyes.

Marie pats the quilt down around his shoulders and washes all the dirty dishes she can find and straightens up the living room, which doesn't take long. Alvin is as neat as she is. She doesn't want to leave. She writes her home number by the kitchen phone, wraps the baguettes in foil so they can be reheated, and meets her sons and her husband at the softball game, thinking of Alvin's wet white face, and she cheers whenever Henry cheers.

After he gets over the flu, Alvin won't let Marie pay for her haircuts, or for the coloring she finally agrees to. They are friends, and he is going to make her beautiful. Marie comes home with shining mahogany hair shot with copper highlights, cut short to show off her slender neck, and the women at work say she looks completely different. Henry says he never knew she had such a pretty neck. Alvin even leaves in a few silver strands so that no one will think she dyes her hair. On Wednesdays they have lunch together in the back of the shop, and on Sundays Marie assists Alvin with the brides and the mothers of the brides. She hands him bobby pins and rattail combs and spritzes hairspray so clear and strong you could keep a full head of hair standing straight up if that was the look you were after. Alvin teaches her to do chignons and twists and french braids and to arrange white flowers in the bride's hair. All the women are happy, despite their nervousness, and very, very grateful to Alvin and Marie.

Alvin says, "The next van is going to say 'Alvin and Marie's Wedding on Wheels.'"

Marie has fallen in love with beauty. Henry notices that she has stopped going to Mass, but he doesn't say anything; he doesn't mind, since helping Alvin makes her happier than church ever did. She looks better too. Marie has no occasion to go back to Alvin's apartment, and he never comes to her house.

One Sunday morning Marie is running late and Alvin rings the doorbell. Henry, in his black velour robe and bare legs, opens the door. Although Henry has never even wondered about Alvin's appearance, he knows immediately who he is. Alvin thinks Henry looks just the way he thought he would, maybe a little grayer, just as handsome.

"Come on in, she's almost ready," Henry says. "Coffee?"

"Coffee'd be great. I've got a bride, a mother of a bride, and two bridesmaids waiting for me in Laurel Springs. Hair *and* make-up. You don't want to get into that without coffee. Intravenous bourbon wouldn't hurt."

Henry laughs, surprised. He didn't expect Alvin to sound like such a regular guy. "Come into the kitchen. I was just making a cup."

"Nice house. Marie said you designed it."

"Yeah. When we moved down here, we saw this lot. It came out all right. My father's in construction too, we did the work ourselves. No point paying someone else to screw it up."

"Right. I'd rather do for myself too. I worked in someone else's shop for two years, that was enough for me."

Henry is suddenly glad to be pouring a cup of coffee for Alvin, a fellow entrepreneur and probably a tough little bastard in his own way.

Marie comes running down the stairs just as Alvin is taking his first sip of coffee.

"Hi." Alvin doesn't stand up and kiss her cheeks, the way he always does, and Marie is so hurt she wants to slap them both, sitting there like the Goombah Brothers.

"I'm ready," she says, jamming her hands into the pockets of the fawn suede jacket Alvin told her to buy. "Let's go, Alvin."

"Let the guy finish his coffee, honey. You two have a big morning ahead of you. You want another cup?"

Shut your face, she thinks. Alvin takes two more quick swallows and winks at Marie.

"Let's do it. Henry, thanks for the coffee. Good to meet you."

"Same here."

They shake hands while Marie finds herself rocked by feelings that make no sense to her.

"'Bye, honey," Henry says, lifting one big hand to wave to her.

"'Bye," Marie mumbles, forcing herself to wave back. "The boys won't be home until two."

Henry smiles and reaches for the newspaper as they leave. The house is his.

"I love that jacket on you," Alvin says as he pulls the car into traffic.

"You do? I'm glad you made me get it, everyone loves it and it is the softest thing. Okay with these pants?"

If Marie had her way, Alvin would lay out her clothes every morning. They don't talk about Henry.

When the invitation to the International Stylists' Convention comes, Alvin hands it to Marie.

"Come on, we're going to Miami. You'll be my tax-deductible guest. Get a little sun, mambo at night. You have to come, I can't do it without you."

"Do you really mambo?"

"Darling, you are looking at the Latin Ballroom King of Jersey City."

"All right, tell me what to pack," says Marie, wondering what Henry will have to say about this, seeing herself dancing with Alvin beneath the Miami moon.

The lobby is a white and silver cavern, with plexiglass stalactites spiraling down to meet the tips of silver-sprayed palm trees bearing sparkling white coconuts. Alvin begins laughing in the lobby and is still grinning when they are shown to their adjoining ice-blue rooms, both accented with raspberry flamingos etched in the mirrors and appliquéd onto their queen-size bedspreads.

Alvin and Marie have a ball. Every night Alvin does her hair a little differently and lays out her clothes. The second night, as she is watching in the mirror, Alvin picks up her turquoise silk dress and begins to cha-cha around the room with it, a Latin Fred Astaire.

"Just my color, don't you think?"

Marie can tell that there is something he needs to hear. "It does go with your eyes, I guess turquoise *is* your color."

He blows her a kiss, and they go out to eat stone crabs and drink just one Mai Tai apiece. When Marie is out with Henry, there's always a big fuss over the wine list, and she has to have a glass of something bitter and flat so that he can enjoy the other three glasses. Henry makes fun of her daiquiris and Singapore Slings.

After their triumphant Botticelli bridal arrangement, Alvin orders room service champagne, and as they sit on the tiny terrace, he toasts her.

"To my darling Marie, the most beautiful woman in North Carolina."

Marie blushes with pleasure and looks down at the hem of her ivory dressing gown.

"What would you like?" Alvin asks, his voice so soft that Marie isn't sure what he's saying.

"I have everything I want. This has been the most wonderful three days of my life, and I owe it all to you."

Alvin smiles and kisses her hand.

"What would you like?" she asks, knowing that whatever he says, she wants to give it to him. Even if what he wants is sex, she wants to give it to him, never mind Henry, never mind her own well-known lack of interest, which is at this very moment dissolving.

Alvin tells her that what he wants is to dress in her clothes, in her lingerie, that she is so beautiful he wants to feel what it is to be her, to be even closer to her. He looks right into her eyes at first, but he ends by looking down into the courtyard. Marie has no idea what to say, she refuses even to think the hurtful words that Henry would use. Whatever Alvin wants, she wants to give him. She nods her head, hoping that that is enough.

Alvin walks over to the dresser and takes out a chemise and a half slip and a pair of pantyhose. Marie watches the waves beyond the terrace. She doesn't trust her own face.

Alvin goes into the bathroom, wanting not to frighten Marie, wanting not to embarrass either one of them. He knows what he needs to do. Slowly, he sweeps foundation up from his jawline, over his high cheekbones, all the way back to his ears, making sure there's no line on his neck. He takes out a new, sharp-edged pink lipstick, brushes on one coat, presses a Kleenex to his lips, and puts on a second coat to last. He

Only You

doesn't do much with his small blue eyes, just a little dark
brown mascara and the pale rose eye shadow he's taught
Marie to use, to make her eyes look brighter. He passes the
blush-on brush over his cheeks lightly.

Alvin pauses, looking at himself, closing his eyes a little.
There's so much he can't fix, can't fix right now, anyway. He
takes out the wig he bought in Germany five years ago, six
hundred dollars' worth of beautiful long blond hair, no frizzy
polyester, just some young fraulein's decision to go short one
summer, and there it was. He puts on the pantyhose and the
half-slip and the matching chemise he had persuaded Marie to
buy, hoping that he would be wearing it with her. He wraps
his navy silk robe around him and finds the navy silk mules he
got while picking out the ivory ones for Marie. He loves
Marie's small round feet and spares himself the sight of his
own well-shaped but too large feet sliding into the heels. If he
wore anything larger than a ten, he would go barefoot rather
than be one of those jumbo transvestites, big-knuckled hands
made pathetic by pale pink nail polish, thick necks hidden by
carefully tossed scarves. Alvin lets himself think only about
Marie, about how much she loves him and admires him. He
knows she does. You can fake a lot of things, Alvin knows, but
you can't fake love. He adjusts the wig quickly, tucking up his
light brown bangs, and walks out of the bathroom, away from
the mirror, toward Marie.

Marie has turned down the lights and drawn the sheer
white curtains closed. In the gold, shining moonlight, Alvin
really looks, for one moment, like a pretty woman, strong-
shouldered, with a narrow waist and long legs under her
rustling silk robe.

"You look beautiful," Marie says.

"Marie, angel, right now, I feel beautiful. I feel like you. You know I think you're a beautiful, beautiful woman. I want us to be closer. I want to be very close, okay?"

They look at each other directly, breathing uncertainty and tenderness. Alvin kneels down, carefully, hoping he won't tip over in his heels, and he removes Marie's ivory slippers. He takes her by the hand and lays her down on the bedspread. Marie relaxes a little more; when Henry wants to make love, he always pulls the covers back.

Marie cannot stand to watch Alvin's lipsticked mouth moving down her breast, but she responds to its warm shape, pressing and gently tugging. The muscles in her back ripple, and her brown hair flutters like the leaves of a small bronze tree in the wind. As the tips of his long blond hair brush lightly across her chest, Alvin looks up just in time to see Marie's slight, astonished smile, and he pulls her closer, opening her robe.

"Beautiful," he whispers.

"Beautiful," she says.

Light Breaks
Where No Sun Shines

I didn't expect to find myself in the back of Mr. Klein's store, wearing only my undershirt and panties, surrounded by sable.

"Sable is right for you, Suseleh," Mr. Klein said, draping a shawl-collared jacket over me. "Perfect for your skin and your eyes. A million times a day the boys must tell you. Such skin."

No one except Mr. Klein had ever suggested that my appearance was pleasing. My mother, who was small and English and had decorated half the houses on Long Island with small English cachepots and porcelain dogs, bought me clothes at Lord & Taylor's Pretty Plus and looked the other way when the saleswomen dragged me out in navy blue A-line dresses and plaid jumpers. My eyes, which are almond-shaped and dark, were concealed by grimy pink-framed glasses, and my creamy, rolling flesh was too much a reminder of dead Romanian relatives and attic photographs to be appealing.

I stood on a little velvet footstool and modeled fur coats for Mr. Klein. He had suggested I take off my perpetual green corduroys and hooded sweatshirt so we could see how the coats really looked. I agreed, only pretending to hesitate for a minute so I could watch his thin gray face expand and pinken. I felt the warm rushing in my chest that being with him gave me. He also gave me Belgian chocolate, because he felt Hershey's wasn't good enough for me, and he told me that if only God had blessed him and Mrs. Klein with a wonderful daughter like me, he would be truly happy, *kayn ahora*. My mother never said I was wonderful. My father, who greatly admired my mother for her size and her accent, was not heard to thank God for giving him the gift of me.

"This one next, Suseleh." Mr. Klein handed me a small mink coat and set a mink beret on my unwashed hair.

"This is my size. Do kids wear mink coats?"

If you had to dress up, mink was the way to go. Much better than my scratchy navy wool, designed to turn chubby Jewish girls into pale Victorian wards. The fur brushed my chin, and without my glasses (Mr. Klein and I agreed that it was a shame to hide my lovely eyes and so we put my glasses in his coat pocket during our modeling sessions), I felt glamorously Russian. I couldn't see a thing. He put the beret at a slight angle and stepped back, admiring me in my bare feet and my mink.

"Perfect. This is how a fur coat should look on a girl. Not some little stick girl in rabbit. This is an ensemble."

I turned around to see what I could of myself from the back: a brown triangle topped by a white blur and another smudge of brown.

I modeled two more coats, a ranch mink, which displeased Mr. Klein with its careless stitching, and a fox cape, which made us both smile. Even Mr. Klein thought floor-length silver fox was a little much.

As always, he turned his back as I pulled on my jeans and sweatshirt. I sat down on one of the spindly pink velvet chairs, putting my sneakers on as he put away the coats.

We said nothing on the drive home. I ate my chocolate and Mr. Klein turned on WQXR, the only time I have ever listened to classical music with pleasure. Mr. Klein rounded my driveway, trying to look unconcerned. I think we both always expected that one Monday my parents would come rushing out of the house, appalled and avenging.

I went inside, my shoelaces flapping against the hallway's glazed, uneven brick. Could anything be less inviting than a brick foyer? It pressed into the soles of my feet, and every dropped and delicate object shattered irretrievably.

I don't remember which cleaning lady greeted me. We seemed to alternate between elderly Irish women who looked as though they'd been born to rid the world of lazy people's private filth, and middle-aged Bolivian women quietly stalking dust and fingerprints. I cannot remember the face that came out of the laundry room to acknowledge my existence, but I know someone let me in. I didn't have a house key until I was nineteen.

Every dinner was a short horror; my eating habits were remarked upon, and then my mother would talk about politics and decorating. My father's repertoire was more limited. He talked about his clients, their divorces, and their bank accounts. I would go to my room, pretend to do my homework, and read my novels. In my room, I was the Scarlet Pimpernel. Sometimes I was Sydney Carton, and once in a while I was Tarzan. I went to sleep dreaming of the nineteenth century, my oldest, largest teddy bear held tightly between my legs.

Mr. Klein lived two houses down and usually drove up beside me as I was walking to the bus stop. Every time I saw the hood of his huge, unfashionable blue Cadillac slide slowly by me and pause, I would skip ahead and throw my books into the front seat, spared another day of riding the school bus. If you have been an outcast, you understand what the bus ride was like. If you have not been, you will think that I'm exaggerating, even now, and that I should have spent less time being sorry for myself and more time being friendly.

He dropped me off in front of Longview Elementary School as the buses discharged all the kids I had managed to avoid thus far. The mornings Mr. Klein failed to appear, I kept a low profile and worried about him until the routine of school settled upon me, vulnerable again only during recess. The first two days of kindergarten had taught me always to carry a book, and as soon I found a place on the hardtop, I had only to set my eyes upon the clean black letters and the soft ivory page and I would be gone, spirited right out of what passed for my real life.

Our first trip to Furs by Klein was incidental, barely a foreshadowing of our afternoons together. Mr. Klein had passed me on the way home from school. Having lost two notebooks since school began, I'd missed the bus while searching the halls frantically for my third, bright red canvas designed to be easily seen. I walked home, a couple of miles through the sticky, smoky leaf piles and across endless emerald lawns. No one knew I liked to walk. Mr. Klein pulled up ahead of me and signaled shyly. I ran to the car, gratified to tears by a smile that I could see from the road.

"I'll give you a ride home, but I need to stop back at my shop, something I forgot. All right?"

I nodded. It was better than all right; maybe I'd never have to go home. He could have driven me to Mexico, night after night over the Great Plains, and I wouldn't have minded.

Furs by Klein stood on the corner of Shore Drive, its curved, pink-tinted windows and black lacquered French doors the height of suburban elegance. Inside stood headless bodies, six rose velvet torsos, each wearing a fur coat. There were mirrors everywhere I looked, and a few thin-legged, armless chairs. The walls were lined with coats and jackets and capes. Above them, floating on transparent necks, were the hats.

Mr. Klein watched me. "Go ahead," he said. "All ladies like hats." He pulled a few down and walked discreetly into the workroom at the rear. I tried on a black cloche with a dotted veil and then a kelly green fedora with a band of arching brown feathers. Mr. Klein emerged from the back, his hands in the pockets of his baggy gray trousers.

"Come, Susie, your mother will be worried about you. Leave the hats, it's all right. Mondays are the day off, the girls will put them back tomorrow." He turned out the lights and opened the door for me.

"My mother's not home." I'm really an orphan, adopt me.

"Tcha, I am so absentminded. Mrs. Klein tells me your mother is a famous decorator. Of course, she is out—decorating."

He smiled, just slightly, and I laughed out loud. He was on my side.

Almost every morning now, he gave me a ride to school. And without any negotiating that I could recall, I knew that on Monday afternoons I would miss my bus and he would pick me up as I walked down Baker Hill Road. I would keep him company while he did whatever he did in the back room, and I would try on hats. After a few Mondays, I eyed the coats.

"Of course," he said. "When you're grown up, you'll tell

your husband, 'Get me a sable from Klein's. It's Klein's or nothing.'" He waggled a finger sternly, showing me who I would be: a pretty young woman with a rich, indulgent husband. "Let me help you."

Mr. Klein slipped an ash blond mink jacket over my sweatshirt and admired me aloud. Soon after, he stopped going into the workroom, and soon after that, I began taking off my clothes. The pleasure on Mr. Klein's face made me forget everything I had heard in the low tones of my parents' conversation and all that I had seen in my own mirror. I chose to believe Mr. Klein.

At home, to conjure up the feeling of Mr. Klein's cool, round fingertips on my shoulders, touching me lightly before the satin lining descended, I listened to classical music. My father made vaguely approving noises from behind the *Wall Street Journal.*

I lay on the floor of the living room, behind the biggest couch, and saw myself playing the piano, adult and beautifully formed. I am wearing a dress I saw on Marilyn Monroe, the sheerest clinging net, with sparkling stones coming up over the tips of my breasts and down between my legs. I am moving slowly across the stage, the wide hem of my sable cape shaping a series of round, dark waves. I hand the cape to an adoring Mr. Klein, slightly improved and handsomely turned out in a tuxedo cut just like my father's.

My mother stepped over me and then stopped. I was eye to toe with her tiny pink suede loafers and happy to stay that way. Her round blue eyes and her dread of wrinkles made her stare as harsh and haunting as the eyeless Greek heads she put in my father's study.

"How are you keeping busy, Susan?"

I couldn't imagine what had prompted this interest. My

126

mother always acted as though I had been raised by a responsible and affectionate governess, and guilt and love were as foreign in my house as butter and sugar.

"School, books." I studied the little gold bars across the tongues of her loafers.

"And that's all going well?"

"Fine. Everything's fine."

"You wouldn't like to study an instrument, would you? Piano? We could do a piano in the library. That could be attractive. An older piece, deep browns, a maroon paisley shawl, silver picture frames. Quite attractive."

"I don't know. Can I think about it?" I didn't mind being part of my mother's endless redecorating; in the past, her domestic fantasies had produced a queen-size brass bed, which I loved and kept into adulthood, and a giant dollhouse, complete with working lights and a chiming doorbell.

"Of course, think it over. Let's make a decision next week, shall we?" She started to touch my dirty hair and patted me on the shoulder instead. I have no idea what she thought of me.

I didn't see Mr. Klein until the following Monday. I had endured four mornings at the bus stop: leaves stuffed down my shirt, my books knocked into the trash can, my lunch bag tossed from boy to boy. Fortunately, the bus driver was a madman, and his rageful mutterings and obscene limericks captured whatever attention might have come my way once we were on the bus.

It was raining that Monday, and I wondered if I should take the bus. I had never thought about the fact that Mr. Klein and I had no way to contact each other. I could only wait, in silence. I pulled up my hood and started walking down Baker Hill, waiting for a blue streak to come past my left side, waiting for the slight skid of wet leaves as Mr. Klein braked to a stop. Finally, much closer to home than usual, the car came.

"You're almost home," he said. "Maybe I should just take you home? We can go to the store another time." He looked rushed and unhappy.

"Sure, if you don't have time, that's okay."

"I have the time, Susie. I have the time." He turned the car around and drove us back to Furs by Klein.

I got out and waited in the rain while he unlocked the big black doors.

"You're soaking wet," he said harshly. "You should have taken the bus."

"I missed it," I lied. If he wasn't going to admit that he wanted me to miss the bus, I wasn't going to admit that I had missed it for him.

"Yes, you miss the bus, I pick you up. Suseleh, you are a very special girl, and standing around an old man's shop in wet clothes is not what you should be doing."

Usually what I did was stand around with no clothes on at all, but I could tell that Mr. Klein, like most adults, was now working only from his version of the script.

I sat down uneasily at the little table with the swiveling gilt-framed mirror, ready to try on hats. Without Mr. Klein's encouragement, I wouldn't even look at the coats. He didn't hand me any hats.

He pressed his thin sharp face deep into the side of my neck, pushing my sweatshirt aside with one hand. I looked in the mirror and saw my own round wet face, comic in its surprise and pink glasses. I saw Mr. Klein's curly gray hair and a bald spot I would never have discovered otherwise.

"Get your coat." He rubbed his face with both hands and went to the door.

"I don't have a coat."

"They let you go in the rain, with no coat? *Gottenyu*. Let's go, please." He held the door open for me, and I had to walk through it.

The chocolate wasn't my usual Belgian slab. It was a deep gold foil box, tied with pink and gold wisps and crowned with a cluster of sparkling gold berries. He dropped it in my lap like it was something diseased.

I held the box in my lap, stroking the fairy ribbons, until he told me to open it.

Each of the six chocolates had a figure on top. Three milk, three bittersweet, each one carved with angel wings or a heart or a white-rimmed rose. In my parents' fat-free home, my eating habits were regarded as criminal. They would no more have bought me beautiful chocolates than gift-wrapped a gun for a killer.

"Suseleh . . . "

He looked out the window at the rain and I looked up at him quickly. I had obviously done something wrong, and although my parents' anger and chagrin never bothered me a bit, his unhappiness pulled me apart. I crushed one of the chocolates with my fingers, and Mr. Klein saw me.

"Nah, nah, nah," he said softly, wiping my fingers with his handkerchief. He cleared his throat. "My schedule's changing, I won't be able to give you rides after school. I'm going to open the shop on Mondays."

"How about in the morning?" I had not known that I could talk through this kind of pain.

"I don't think so. I need to get in a little earlier. It's not so bad, you should ride with other boys and girls. You'll see, you'll have a good time."

I sat there sullenly, ostentatiously mashing the chocolates.

"Too bad, they're very nice chocolates. Teuscher's. Remember, sable from Klein's, chocolates from Teuscher's. Only the best for you. I'm telling you, only the best."

"I'm not going to have a good time on the bus." I didn't mash the last chocolate, I just ran a fingertip over the tiny ridges of the rosebud.

"Maybe not. I shouldn't have said you'd have a good time. I'm sorry." He sighed and looked away.

I bit into the last chocolate. "Here, you have some too."

"No, they're for you. They were all for you."

"I'm not that hungry. Here." I held out the chocolate half and he lowered his head, startling me. I put my fingers up to his narrow lips and he took the chocolate neatly between his teeth. I could feel the very edge of his teeth against my fingers.

We pulled up in front of my house, and he put his hand over mine, for just one moment.

"I'll say it again, only the best is good enough for you. So, we'll say au revoir, Susan. Not good-bye."

"Au revoir. Thank you for the chocolates." My mother's instructions surfaced at odd times.

I left my dripping sneakers on the brick floor and dropped my wet clothes into the lilac straw hamper in my bathroom. I took my very first voluntary shower and dried off slowly, watching myself in the steamy mirror. When I didn't come down for dinner, my mother found me, naked and quiet, deep in my covers.

"Let's get the piano," I said.

I took lessons from Mr. Canetti for three years, and he served me wine-flavored cookies instead of chocolate. One day, he bent forward to push my sleeves back over my aching wrists, and I saw my beautiful self take shape in his eyes. I loved him, too.

Semper Fidelis

I shop at night. Thursday nights I wave good-bye to the nurse and drive off, feigning reluctance. The new mall has three department stores, a movie theater, and hundreds of little shops, and I have been in all but the Compleat Sportsman. It makes no sense to me, but I cannot sit through a movie, knowing I'm supposed to be shopping. I eat warm peanut butter cookies and wander around for almost two hours, browsing through the very slim jazz sections of the mall record stores, skimming bestsellers. At nine-thirty, when the mall is closing and it's just me and the vagrant elderly and the young security guards, I go grocery shopping.

All-night grocery stores seem to be the personal savior and favorite haunt of dazed young women of all colors, who haul their crumpled, sleeping babies like extra items in the cart; of single middle-aged men and women, too healthy and too lonely to fall asleep at ten o'clock; and of people like me, who are scared to go home. It is my belief, and sometimes my wish, that my husband will die while I am out on one of my Thursday night sprees.

Max and I have been together for almost ten years, since I was eighteen and he was fifty. We are no longer a scandal, or a tragedy. His wife's friends and the other witnesses have moved away, or fallen silent, or become friends, the limited choices of a small town. Max and I are close to ordinary, made interesting only by our past and its casualties. Women who would have, may have, spit in my soup at painfully quiet dinner parties ten years ago now bring puréed vegetables for Max and articles on the apricot-pit clinics of Mexico. I have become a wife, soon to be a widow, and I feel more helpless and unknowing after ten years of marriage than I was at eighteen, moving into Max's apartment with two t-shirts, a box of records, and no shoes. On our first outing, Max introduced me to the chairman of his department and bought me sneakers.

He has not been out of bed for three weeks, and he has not spoken since morning. I always pictured myself as an Audrey Hepburn–type widow, long-necked and pale in a narrow black linen dress. Instead, I am nearly drowning in a river of sugar and covering myself in old sweatpants and Max's flannel shirts. I only dress up on Thursday nights, to go out in an oversized sweatshirt and black tights, playing up my legs with high-heeled black ankle boots. I have never dressed like this in my life, and I am glad to put my sneakers and my jeans back on before I go into the house.

Ray, at the Deli Counter, is the one I've been looking for. He first admired my boots and then my whole outfit, and after three Thursdays in a row I felt obliged to buy another top for him to look at, and he leaned over the counter to tell me how much he liked it and winked as he went back to work. Ray can't be more than twenty-two, and I assume he is a recovering addict of some kind, since he is presently the picture of good health and says things like "Easy does it" and "One day at a time," which are the kinds of things my brother, a not-recovering alcoholic, says whenever he calls to wish me well or borrow money. I think Ray is a good choice. I think we would not discuss poetry or symbolism or chemotherapy or the past, and I think I would have a beer and he would not and I would lay my hand on one thick thigh until I felt the cloth tighten under my fingers, and when we were done I would climb out of his van, or his room in his mother's house, and thank him from the bottom of my heart and go home to Max.

I come home to see the nurse leaning over Max, smoothing his covers as her big white nylon breasts swing slightly and shadow his face. He smiles, and I see that he is unaware of my presence and the nurse is not.

"The pearls," she says, continuing their conversation, "were extremely valuable, and irregardless of the will, my sister and I both think the pearls should have come to us. Our mother's pearls should have come to us, because they were already ours."

I cannot even begin to understand what she's talking about, but it feels ominously metaphorical. Maybe the pearls represent Max's health, or his first marriage, or our vow to cleave unto each other: things irretrievably gone and valued more in their absence than in their presence. I want to shut her up, to keep her from tormenting us both, but Max smiles again, a quick softening of his bony gray face, and even I can see that he is not tormented. I knock against the door frame, knowing that Max, as he is now, is too innocent and the nurse too self-absorbed to appreciate the irony of my knocking. I am performing without an audience, which is how it has been for some time. If you feel sorry for yourself, can it still be a tragedy? Or are you reduced to a rather unattractive second lead, a foil for the heroes, blind and beautiful, courageously polishing the brass as the icy waters lap at their ankles? It seems to me—and I would not be sorry to find out—that I have disappeared.

"Sweetheart," he says, and the nurse frowns.

"He's been asking for you," she says, and I forgive her bitchiness because she seems to care about him, to feel that it matters that he misses me. The other nurses are solicitous of his health, of his illness, but his feelings are nothing more than symptoms to them. For one minute, I love her for loving him; he has made me love people I would dislike if he were going to live.

"Dawn's mother passed away recently, she was telling me."

Shaken by love, touched by his effort to keep us together and to keep us his, I smile at Dawn. "I'm so sorry," I say, trying to be good. "I lost my mother just last year. And I've got a sister too." That's it. I cannot think of any more astonishing coincidences that will bring us together.

"My sister's my best friend," Dawn says, sitting in the armchair near the bed as though she'd dropped in on Max for a visit.

"Mine, too." Amazing. Dawn and I must have been separated at birth.

My sister, Irene, *is* my best friend, and while my father wept and my mother murmured congratulations from the far side of a scotch and soda, my sister took me upstairs, to what had been her room, to discuss my marrying Max.

"You can have anyone, you know. Even after all this. You can transfer to a school in California and no one will ever know. You don't have to marry him."

"I love him, Reen. I want to marry him."

"Okay. Okay, I'll be there. At least he won't leave you for a younger woman. Not without being arrested. Is this justice of the peace or train-and-veil?"

"Justice of the peace. Wednesday."

"All right. How about a suit? Silk suit, roses in your hair? It won't kill you to go to a beauty parlor."

And my sister got my legs waxed, my pores cleaned, and my eyebrows shaped in less than forty-eight hours. In the photographs, I look radiant and only a little too young for the ivory silk suit, which Irene found, unpinned from a mannequin, and paid for in less than forty-five minutes. I have ivory roses in my upswept black hair, and Max is laughing at the camera, which is held by his oldest friend, who is astonished, amiable, and drunk for the whole afternoon. My sister looks like the mother of the bride, exhausted, vigilant, more pleased than not. My parents weren't there because I didn't invite them, despite Max's pleas.

I should have invited them. I am almost thirty now and I am coming to think that one should, when in doubt, invite them, whoever they are. The distant relatives, the cocktail party stalwarts, the friends who failed to send Christmas cards two years in a row. Invite them while you can.

Dawn rises to leave, and I can see that she doesn't love Max; he is just a better than average case, less trouble than some of the others. I am free to hate her, and I walk her to the door and open it for her, without speaking, a form of civilized rudeness I've picked up from my mother.

"Come here," Max says, but I cannot lie in that bed.

"I'll use the cot." When we left the hospital, a smart, angry woman in the support group told me to get a cot and didn't even pretend to listen when I said that we would continue to share a bed.

"Undress slowly, sweetheart. I can still look."

In the books I keep hidden, the guides to grief, the how-to

books of widowhood and the period that comes before, the authors mention, delicately, that the healthy spouse usually suffers hurt feelings and frustration due to the dying person's lack of sexual interest. This doesn't seem to be the case with Max.

I throw off my clothes and lie on the cot, like a Girl Scout, still in my t-shirt, panties, and socks. I hear a wet, bubbling noise, which is how he laughs now.

Max rests one cool, brittle hand on my stomach.

"How was the supermarket?"

"It was okay. I got some groceries."

"And the mall?"

"It was fine. I got some socks."

He strokes my stomach with just two dry fingertips, and I feel the flesh at the end of each finger, dragging slightly after the bone. I want to throw up and I want to weep.

"Do you ever meet anybody?"

"Like who?" I ask. Despite everything, I don't think of Max as a jealous man; we have simply misunderstood each other most of the time. He would remind me, as we drove home from parties, that he had made a point of not admiring the younger women so people wouldn't think that I was part of his youth fetish, that I was less than unique. He said I owed him the same consideration and should conceal my impulsive sexuality lest people think that my marriage to him was just hormonally-driven adolescent mindlessness. We agreed, many times, that he was not jealous, not insecure, not possessive, and we must have had that conversation about flirting a hundred times in our ten years together.

Max pokes me lightly. "I don't know, like anybody. Some nice young man?"

"No. No one." I roll over on my side, out of reach of his fingers.

"All right, don't get huffy. Dawn gave me my meds already. Good night, sweetheart."

"Good night." You sadistic old shit.

I lie on the cot, listening to his chalky, irregular breath until he falls asleep, and then I go downstairs to pay bills. His room, our room, fills up at night, with a thick wet mist of dark fluids and invisibly leaking sores. This is something else I don't say.

The next Thursday I smile encouragingly at Ray, who is very busy with the second-shift shopping crowd. I find myself taking a number behind a dark, dark boy, so dark the outline of his whole brown body seems drawn in charcoal. He is all roundness, high, full Island cheeks, round black eyes, rounded arms and shoulders, his pants rounded front and back. My own fullness has begun to shrink and loosen, muscle sliding down from bone a little more each year. I want to cut this boy open like a melon, and eat him, slice by slice. Cut him and taste him and have him and hurt him. I could tell Max that I understand him better now than I did ten years ago, but he would be horrified that I think this mixture of lust and resentment is anything like his love for me. I am only horrified by myself; what I want to do to this boy, Max would never do.

Ray and I exchange several devoted, affectionate glances; as aspiring lovers we are so tenderly playful and wistful it seems odd that all we really want is to fuck each other senseless and get home before we're caught. My attitude is not good.

I go home to Max and Dawn. She is in my kitchen, sipping tea out of my mermaid mug, a gift from Max after a terrible, rainy week on Block Island. The iridescent blue tail is the handle, and Dawn's smooth fingers cling to it.

After she leaves, Max questions me again.

"I don't meet anyone, for Christ's sake. I'm not a girl. I'm twenty-eight and I probably look ninety. Who would I meet?"

"You might meet anyone. Look at me. I'm sixty. I'm a dying man riddled with cancer, and I met Dawn."

"Great. I hope you'll be very happy together." I turn out the light so he cannot see me change, and I wonder if he gets Dawn to strip for him on Thursdays.

"Really," he says, completely surrounded by pillows so he can't lie down and be engulfed by his own lungs. "Tell me. Why shouldn't you meet someone?"

I try to see him in the dark as he is, everything that was broad and hard-boned now transparent at the edge, softly dimpled and concave at the center.

"Who would I meet?"

"Some good-looking young man at the mall. Not a salesman, you never like salesmen. They try too hard, don't they?"

"Yes." I want to tell him to rest, but I don't think I would be saying it for him.

"Big and dark. Sweet-natured, not terribly bright. Not stupid, of course, but not intellectual. Not an academic. I want to spare you a long, pedantic lecture when you've only got a few hours."

"Good idea. How long do I have?"

"Well, you know your schedule better than I. Two hours at the mall, an hour and a half at the supermarket. We can skip aerobics, I think. I cannot picture you with a man who goes to aerobics class."

He's right. I like them big and burly or lean and lithe, but I cannot bear the compulsively athletic, the ones who measure their pulses and their biceps and their cholesterol levels.

"Tell me, sweetheart. Tell me about the man you met in the supermarket."

"Not the mall?"

"Don't play games with me. Tell me what happened."

"He's dark-haired but fair. Black Irish and big. Not tall but wide. Built like a wall." I realize that I am describing the Max I have seen only in photographs, a big, wild boy with one cocky foot on his Army jeep; ramming his way through Harvard a few years later, grinning like a pirate as the wind blows both ends of his scarf behind him.

"Go on," Max says.

"I do see him at the supermarket. I change my clothes to go there." And I tell Max the truth about my clothes, and he says "Ya-*hoo*" when I come to the black ankle boots. We are having some kind of fun, in this terrible room.

"That'll get him. Do you wear a bra?"

"Come on, Max, of course I wear a bra."

"Just slows you down. All right, at least it's one of your pretty ones, I hope, not those Ace Bandage things. How about the purple and black one with the little cutouts?" Max likes silky peekaboo lingerie, and I buy it, but I do not wear seventy-dollar hand-finished bras and garter belts for everyday. Most of the time, I wear cheap cotton tubes, which he hates.

"I do wear the black and purple one."

"And the panties?"

"No panties."

"Wonderful. The first time I put my hand on your bare ass, I thought I had died and gone to heaven. And then I was afraid that it wasn't for me, that you just never wore them."

"Max, you asked me not to wear them, remember? I always wore underpants." I'd had some sex, more than enough, with boys and by myself when I met Max, but I had never had a lover. Everything important that I know, about literature, about people, about my own body, I have learned from this man, and he is leaving me the way we both expected I would leave him, loving, regretful, irretrievable.

"Tell me about this big guy."

"Big guy" is what I used to call Max. Having been married to a woman who called him "my dear," and pursued by highly educated young women who called him Professor Boyle and thought he was God, he found terms like "big guy" and "butch" refreshing endearments.

"He's the night manager." I have given Ray a promotion; I'm sure, in time, someone with his good looks and pleasant manner will be made manager, and a sexual encounter with Ray the Head Roast Beef Slicer seems to demean us all.

"Fine. Where did you do it?"

"Jesus, Max, what is wrong with you?"

"Need you ask? Come on, come on, don't get skittish now. Where did you do it?" That angry, pushing voice used to scare me to death, and I cannot bear that it doesn't scare me anymore.

"We went to Wadsworth Park." Where Max and I used to go when I was still living with my parents and he was still living with his then-wife. Just recently, while sorting out his pills or shaving his distorted face, I find myself thinking, This is what a wife is. Now that we cannot see ourselves in the curious, excited eyes of other people, the differences that defined us are fading away. We are just a man who is dying and a woman who is not.

"A little buggy?"

"Not too bad." I stall to avoid making a mistake, afraid that I am not telling the right story.

"You had a blanket and you didn't notice the bugs."

"Max, what do you want from me?"

"I want you to tell me what happened when you got into the woods. You led him to those big rocks, by the stream?"

The woods are thick on both sides of the water, sheltering twin slabs of granite. When we were there, Max would press me so far backward that the ends of my hair trailed in the cold water, collecting small leaves as I lay under him.

"All right. We went to the rocks and we made love. Then I changed my clothes and came home."

"Don't tell me like that," he says, and begins to cough, loosely, his whole body bouncing on the plastic-covered mattress. He falls asleep, still coughing, and I go downstairs and do nothing.

For the rest of the week, he floats in and out of conversations, and Dawn turns out to be very good at injections and bed changes, which should not surprise me. On Thursday I put on my shopping costume while Max watches and smiles alertly. Dawn is reading magazines in the kitchen, waiting for me to leave.

"Tonight?" he asks, barely pushing the words through his lips.

I don't answer, just tie my boots and sit down to brush my hair.

"You know who Dawn reminds me of? Not coloring, but the build? Eren Goknar. Remember?"

I remember and I keep brushing my hair.

"I wonder where she is."

"I don't know. Maybe she went back to Turkey."

"Don't think so. She wrote to me from California, teaching at Berkeley. Marvelous girl," he says, struggling with each consonant. I walk out of the room.

I put up some hot water for me and Dawn and go back to check on Max, afraid that he will die while I'm angry with him.

"Ready?"

"Yeah. I'll be back in a couple of hours."

"I slept with Eren," he says, and sighs.

"I know," I say, although I hadn't known until then. And I know that he is pushing me away, furiously, as though I will miss him less because he had sex with Eren Goknar. He can no more lose me than I can lose myself, we are like those house keys that beep in response to your voice; they practically find you. I kiss the air near Max's face and return to Dawn, who has made tea. We chat for two hours, in between her runs upstairs, and she doesn't ask me why I don't go out. I send her home at eleven.

Max barely opens his eyes when I turn on the night-light to undress. He lifts one hand slightly and I go to him, still in my underwear.

"Off," he whispers. He turns his head and coughs, the harsh, rude sound of a straw in an almost empty glass.

I take everything off and climb into the bed, trying not to press against him now that even the sheets seem to hurt him.

"Did you?"

I slide closer to him until we are face to face, and I kiss his dry lips and feel the small bumps and cracks around his mouth.

"Yes, I found him, the one I told you about. The big one. He was getting off work early, just as I got there. I didn't even have to wait."

Max closes his eyes, and I put his hand on top of my leg.

"It was so dark we didn't go to the park. We went to a

motel. There was tacky red wallpaper, and the bed was a huge heart with a red velvet bedspread."

"Route Sixty-eight," he says.

"That one. Remember that big bed? And the headboard with the little posts, the handholds?"

I move his hand up and down my leg, very gently.

"He undressed me, Max. He knelt down and took off my shoes, and then he laid me on the bed and undressed me. He was still in his suit."

"Suit?" Max whispered.

"His work clothes, I mean. Not a suit. He left the light on and began to kiss me all over, but every time I tried to touch him, he'd grab my hands. He wouldn't let me touch him until later."

Max moves his head a little, to nod, and I prop his pillows up.

"He kissed the insides of my thighs and the backs of my legs, and then he kissed my back for a very long time, and when he turned me over he was undressed. And he pulled me up to him, about two feet in the air, and then he threw us both down on the bed and he came inside me and he just kept coming and coming at me until I started to cry and then we got under the covers and we both cried until we fell asleep."

I lay my wet face next to Max's and listen for his breathing.

"It was the best, Max. Nothing in my life was ever like that. Do you hear me? Nothing in my life was ever like that."

When the Year Grows Old

On a Wednesday afternoon, Kay Feldman came home from Italian Club, which was run by Signora Maselli and filled with other misfits, girls bright enough but too shy for the school paper, too prim or clumsy for Modern Dance, and one boy, obviously crazy, who announced that he planned to read all of Dante before the end of ninth grade. Kay called out for her mother and heard nothing. There was no note on the kitchen table, only half a cup of thickening coffee and an ashtray with stubbed-out cigarettes.

Kay's mother only drank tea, usually herbal tea, and she had never, as far as Kay knew, ever smoked a cigarette. Kay had never even seen an ashtray in their house. When her aunt Ruth came to visit, Kay's father made her go outside to smoke, even in the winter. Kay could feel cold lines of sweat sliding down her sides.

Kay called out again and walked through every room, telling herself that her mother had gone for a walk, which she sometimes did, and had just forgotten to leave a note, which was unimaginable. Kay looked through the rooms of their house, excited beneath her anxiety, wondering whether she would see something terrible. A body, not her mother's, of course, but maybe some anonymous body flung across the bed, murdered by an anonymous someone else. Even better, murdered by her father, who will rot in jail and Kay will change her name and never, ever visit him. There was no body. The beds were unmade, which was unusual, and her mother's typewriter, which sat on a small pine table in what they called the guest room, was missing. Kay heard a faint mewing sound and jumped. Her father claimed he was allergic to cats, and despite her pleas and her mother's wistful looks, there were no pets. Kay didn't think he was allergic at all; she thought, correctly, that he hated cats and didn't want to argue.

The mewing came from the basement. Kay walked down, thinking about herself in the fictional third person, as she sometimes did: "Bravely, Portia Ives descended the creaky stairs into the dank basement ... " The Feldman basement was not particularly dank, as basements go. Her parents would never do anything as suburban or hospitable as finishing off the basement, but it was usually dry, and the only smell was of cool concrete and minerals. At the bottom of the steps, Kay sniffed repeatedly, in disbelief: those confusing, disorienting smells were the sharp reek of cat pee and the ropy, sexy scent of cigarettes.

"Oh, hi, honey, I didn't hear you come in."

Kay's mother was wearing clothes Kay didn't recognize. Her straight blond hair was pushed back by a wide black headband, and she had on a baggy black v-neck sweater, the sleeves pushed up to her elbows. Her pants were black too, and she was barefoot.

"Is there a cat in here?" Kay wanted to grab her mother, shouting, What kind of joke, what kind of demented game is this, cigarettes and cats and the beds not made?

Kay's mother giggled. The giggle was more frightening than the cigarettes. Kay's mother did not giggle; she smiled pleasantly at her husband's elaborate puns, and she pretended not to hear Kay's rude remarks.

"Yes, there is. He's not quite potty-trained, but we're getting there. Did you know that even very small kittens will begin using the kitty litter within twenty-four hours? And they've got this new kind of kitty litter, it's green and it's incredibly absorbent and soaks up most of the smell. He's in the corner there."

"Whose cat is he?" And why are you sitting on a folding chair, in the middle of the afternoon, in the goddamn basement?

"Mine, ours. How about calling him Blake—you know, 'Tyger! Tyger! burning bright / In the forests of the night, / What immortal hand or eye / Could frame thy fearful symmetry?' Do they still teach that at school? I think Blake is still my all-time favorite. I love 'Songs of Experience.'"

Kay stared at her mother. Her mother, the mother she knew, taught English as a Second Language in Adult Education and was always in the kitchen at five o'clock getting dinner started so the kitchen would be clean by the time she went to teach. Kay's mother wore khaki slacks with a narrow brown belt, brown flats, and pink or white turtlenecks. Sometimes she wore navy or mint green. When she went to teach, she put on a skirt and a cardigan with one of the turtlenecks. Kay's father said, trying to be nice, that Laura dressed like a lady. More often, he said she dressed like a nun.

"Where did you get those clothes, Mom?"

Laura looked at Kay in surprise and looked down at her black pants. She shrugged. "I found them in the trunk. I can't believe they still fit. Isn't that nice?"

At least her mother's verbal habits hadn't changed: cheerful evasion, calling everything "nice." Kay decided to act as though nothing else had changed.

"Are you coming upstairs? It's after five."

"I don't think so, honey. I'm in the middle of something, and it's going to take a little longer to get Blake acclimated. Look at him, cowering over there. Do you want to pick him up?"

Kay looked at her mother, who always warned her that animals carry germs, and looked at the kitten, a tiny bundle of strawberry blond spikes. Yesterday, if they had somehow acquired a kitten, her mother would have suggested calling him Sunshine or Buttercup, and Kay would have rolled her eyes in contempt. Kay picked up the kitten and could feel him squirming, brushing the back of her hand with a tongue like a tiny thistle.

"So what am I supposed to do? Do I have to make dinner?"

"Well, no, I wouldn't think so. Didn't you stop at Swenson's? You're not hungry yet, are you?"

Kay was having trouble with the idea that this weird beatnik knew everything her mother knew and seemed to be able to make use of it, in ways her mother was never able to manage.

"No, I guess not. He's going to be really mad, Mom, you know, when dinner's not ready."

Laura looked at her mildly. "Well, it won't be the end of the world if dinner's a little late. How anyone can eat at six, I don't know; it always seemed to me that one had hardly finished lunch. I'll finish what I'm doing and then I'll come up. We can eat around seven. I'm not teaching tonight."

Kay said nothing. In her head, she repeated the airy sound

of "one had hardly finished lunch" and felt a burst of joy blanketing her worries. Perhaps this would be something good, something better than anything had ever been.

Kay heard her father, Martin, come home promptly at six o'clock, as he usually did, and she heard him call out, hiding his surprise, and his immediate anger at being surprised, with a jolly impatience. "Where the hell is everybody?"

Kay lay on her bed, stomach down, and waited for him to find her. He would only hover in her doorway; he rarely came into her bedroom.

"Hi. Where's your mother?"

"She's in the basement."

"Come on, Kay, don't be stupid. I don't have time for it."

Copying her mother's mild tone, Kay said, "She's in the basement."

"For Christ's sake." Her father stalked off.

Kay walked quietly to the top of the basement stairs. She heard her father mumbling angrily, and she heard her mother's voice cut him off so softly no words floated up the stairs. A few minutes later, Martin came up the stairs, uneasy and looking for a fight.

"Did you do your homework?"

"Yes." Kay knew better than to tell him that she had just gotten home.

"All right. Why don't you set the table or something? Your mother said dinner will be a little late."

"No problem."

"You sound like a gas station attendant when you say that. Just say, 'That will be fine,' like a normal, educated person."

In her coldest voice, Kay said, "That will be fine." She thought, And I hate you, you fat, fat, evil pig, and I hope you die.

Kay's mother came up and made hamburgers, mashed pota-toes, and a green salad. She didn't speak during dinner, and the three of them ate in silence, Kay watching them both. Laura put her own dishes in the dishwasher, and as Kay and Martin sat there, she turned to leave.

"Where are you going, Laura?" Martin couldn't move fast enough to block her way, but he wasn't going to sit by while his wife acted like some second-rate Sylvia Plath.

"Downstairs. I'm working on something, and I find that the basement is the most comfortable place. Like your office at the college is for you. Fold-out couch and all."

Martin said nothing, and Kay watched his face turn a slow, swelling red. Her mother didn't stay to watch.

Martin went to read in their bedroom, hoping that tomor-row would find his wife in her usual clothes and her usual mildly depressed state, smelling like baby powder and not cigarettes.

At ten, Kay called downstairs, "I'm going to bed, Mom. I did the dishes. Good night."

"Good night, honey. That was very sweet of you, doing the dishes. I'll be up in a little bit."

"Well, I'm going to bed now." Kay had been ducking her mother's evening attentions for the last four years. Tonight, she wanted to be tucked in, but her mother stayed in the base-ment, resolute, in black.

In the morning, there was a note on the basement door.

Give me, O indulgent fate!
Give me yet, before I die,
A sweet, but absolute retreat
'Mongst paths so lost, and trees so high,
That the world may ne'er invade

Through such windings and such shade
My unshaken liberty.

by Anne Finch,
Countess of Winchilsea

As Kay was reading it for the third time, her father scanned it over her shoulder and then crumpled it and threw it in with the coffee grounds and melon rinds.

That night her mother did not come up to make dinner. Martin went down and made more angry noises and came back up heavily, looking defeated and a little afraid. If Kay hadn't hated his guts, she would have felt sorry for him. Stupid, scared pig.

"Why don't you ask your mother to come upstairs? If she doesn't want to make dinner, we could . . . we could bring in pizza."

Kay didn't want to do anything that could be construed as helping her father, but she did want her mother to come upstairs; wanted her, even more, to witness her father's utter capitulation, to hear "bring in pizza" spoken by the man who had forbidden them to eat at fast-food joints all their lives and had taken all the fun out of family vacations by insisting that Laura cook regular meals every night in whatever cabin kitchen she found herself in.

Kay wanted to shout out, with trumpets and banners, "You can stop now, you've won. He'll bring in pizza, and he hasn't even mentioned the cat. You've won! Come back!"

Kay went downstairs and smelled the smoke and the moth-balls but only a little bit of cat. The typewriter was going steadily.

"Mom?"

"I'm here."

"Dad said why don't we bring in pizza if you don't want to cook. We could get double cheese and peppers." Kay loved double cheese and peppers, and every time Martin went to a conference, Laura would hesitate and then yield, ordering a large for just the two of them, frowning as Kay ate three, then four slices.

When Laura failed to smile triumphantly, Kay's heart sank. It was not a contest, after all.

"If you want to," Laura said, balancing a Dunhill cigarette in the bowl of an unfamiliar crystal ashtray. "This ashtray belonged to my father, you never met him. He was a minor poet and a sweet man. My mother considered him a failure. I always thought so too, but now I think he was just a sweet, soft person, without ambition. Your grandmother admired ambitious men. Do you know what she said to me after she met your father for the first time? She said, 'Get pregnant.'" Laura pulled on her cigarette, looking younger and angrier than Kay had ever seen her.

"Yeah, Grandma was weird. So Mom, the pizza? Should we order it? Just one large? We could get some of the cheese breadsticks too."

"Whatever you want. I'm not hungry."

"Mom, did you eat today?"

"I'm fine, honey. See, Blake's having his dinner." They both looked at the kitten, lapping milk out of a small Wedgwood saucer, which Kay recognized as having come from the set her mother kept on display in their china cabinet.

"Okay, we'll order pizza. Mom, are you sleeping down here?"

"Well, yes, I am. This project is taking up so much time that it seems easier just to get everything set down here. It looks a lot like my room at college."

Kay looked around, unhappy but curious. It looked like the room Kay herself might have when she got to college: Klimt posters taped to the cement walls, a card table covered with two purple batik scarves, a pile of notebooks and a stack of poetry books on the cement floor, curling in the almost unnoticeable damp. Laura had unrolled an old Girl Scout sleeping bag onto the cot and added a few African-looking pillows. She had stacked two boxes of Martin's only book, discounted and autographed, to make an end table, and put a small lamp on top.

"It's nice, Mom."

Her mother beamed at her. "Thank you. 'Let the ambitious rule the earth, / let the giddy fool have mirth, / let me still in my retreat / from all roving thoughts be freed.' That's more of Anne Finch." Her mother looked at her typewriter. "I have to get back to work."

"What are you working on?"

Laura's face closed abruptly. "I'm writing some things. I wrote a lot. I have to get back to work."

"Okay, I'm going. I'll call you when the pizza comes. Okay?"

"Fine." Her mother, who always had ten words for every one of Kay's, pushed up her sleeves and started typing.

Kay and Martin ate pizza together silently. Laura said she was too busy to come up for dinner, and Kay's father ate six slices and threw the box in the garbage. He got his car keys and told Kay to clean up.

"Why should I clean up?"

"Just do it, Kay. I don't know what lunacy your mother is

153

up to, but I can't correct papers, write a book, *and* clean the house."

Kay thought of her mother, luminous in the basement, quoting that woman poet. "I didn't say you should clean the house, did I? I just asked, why I should clean up after the two of us eat."

Martin balled his fists and set them on the table, the picture of a man trying to keep his temper. But he wasn't, Kay knew, he was only trying to scare her.

"Kay, please, clean up the kitchen. Don't make this worse than it is. Don't make me lose my temper. Why don't you go downstairs and get your mother to stop this nonsense? And tell her she has *got* to stop smoking cigarettes."

"I'll clean the kitchen if you're going to threaten me. You tell Mom to stop smoking. She's your wife."

Her father walked out of the kitchen, and Kay could hear that he didn't go out to the car; he went right to the bedroom.

Every day, not knowing what she hoped for, Kay went downstairs to visit her mother. Sometimes Laura was charming and recited poetry, but the next day she might turn weird and slow-moving, hardly able to answer Kay. Martin bought milk and fruit and dinner on his way home every night, and Kay cleaned up the kitchen after they ate the pizza or the fried chicken or the corned beef sandwiches. On the tenth day, Kay went downstairs, not thinking at all about her mother; she was crying because she was fourteen and four inches taller than the only boy who was even a little bit nice to her.

"What's the matter, honey?"

"It was just a shitty day." Since her mother's personality transplant, swearing was now no big deal. Kay was trying to figure out when she could ask for a cigarette.

"They happen." Her mother lit up and leaned back in her

typing chair, turning to look at Kay. "My God, you got so beautiful this year, every time I look at you now I think, 'The brightness of her cheek would shame those stars, / As daylight doth a lamp; her eyes in heaven / Would through the airy region stream so bright / That birds would sing and think it were not night.' You are really just the Juliet. Romeos are a little hard to find in ninth grade, though."

Kay smiled, thrilled to hear her mother, who used to tell her she really could be cute if she smiled more, talk in this quirky, husky voice, a voice of lovers remembered, of disappointments survived.

"No one likes me," Kay said, realizing that at that moment, petting tiny Blake, she didn't care.

"Then they are nearsighted fools and babies. It'll happen, honey. Give everybody two or three more years and you'll be beating them off with a stick, maybe two sticks." Her mother ground out her cigarette for emphasis. "I have to get back to work. Come lie on the cot. You can take a nap while I type."

Kay lay down on the green, dampish sleeping bag and put her head on one of the odd oblong pillows. Her mother pulled the folding chair closer to the cot and put one thin, colorless hand on Kay's shoulder. She sang,

"Oh, the summertime is coming
and the leaves are sweetly blooming
and the wild mountain thyme
grows around the purple heather . . .
Will you go, laddie, go?"

Kay didn't remember that her mother had sung to her nightly in that same breathy, bittersweet voice, rocking her in a small blue bedroom. Her mother sang until Kay fell asleep.

When she woke up, her mother was holding the kitten and staring at the air above the typewriter.

"Mom? Mom?"

The kitten jumped out of Laura's arms and tumbled over to his milk dish.

Kay put a hand on her mother's shoulder, and then both hands; she could feel thin skin shifting over ridges of bone beneath the dirty black sweater. Her mother didn't move, and Kay waited. After a while she could feel a slight heaving.

"What's going on?" Martin stood halfway down the stairs, peering at them, at their two sloping shapes rimmed by the harsh white light. When Kay was born, she could barely stop crying long enough to eat, and Martin would walk her all night, up and down the apartment stairs, while Laura put her head beneath two pillows and cried until dawn. For six months, they all slept on wet sheets. The only picture he had ever carried was of Kay, four months old.

"Nothing," Kay said.

Every day had frightened her more as she waited for her father's move. Obviously, something was wrong with her mother; he could send her away, and she might never come back. He could get rid of Blake, too.

"All right, Kay. Go on upstairs." He sounded the way he always did when he talked to her, as though they were strangers forced to share a seat on a terrible train ride.

Kay stood by her mother.

"Upstairs."

"What are you going to do?" Kay asked, feelings of power, of supernatural strength, surging through her chest. She will rescue her mother the way policemen shimmy through traffic to rescue toddlers, the way acrobats catch each other at the last, impossible half-second. She will swing past her father, leaving him fat and clumsy on the ground, and she and her mother will whirl through light-filled air, landing softly, not even breathing hard, on their own tiny platform.

"I just want to talk to your mother privately."

Kay stood still, squeezing her mother's shoulders, waiting for her cue.

"Martin?" Her mother's voice was softer than the kitten's.

Kay's father came down the stairs, loosening his tie. "It's me, I'm here," he said, and he leaned over the typewriter and took Laura's slack hands.

"Martin?"

Kay waited for her father's explosion, for him to yell at her mother for being stupid and repeating herself. She moved back, just a little, only her fingertips resting on her mother's dusty shoulders.

"Right here, Laura, I'm right here."

"I'm very tired. I'm not sleeping at night."

Her mother's thin whine distracted and annoyed Kay, who was trying hard to turn her into Anne Finch, into a blond, sequined acrobat effortlessly flipping from one shining trapeze to the next.

"I know, I know you can't sleep."

How could he know? Kay thought. Thick and still under his gray, conventional blankets, how could he know what her mother was doing in the night, in the basement?

"Let's go upstairs, Laura, all right? Let's go talk to Sid Schwerner, all right? He can help you sleep."

Laura pulled her hands back angrily, and Kay thought, Now! Leap into my arms, now!

"Martin, I have to get back to work."

Kay's father was smarter than she thought; he didn't yell or even try to take hold of Laura's hands again.

157

"Of course, I didn't mean to interrupt. Let's go meet with Sid, just for a little while, and then you can get back to work. You can't work without rest, right? Even Shakespeare, even Blake, your all-time favorite, they all rested. All right?"

Laura sighed and put her head down on the typewriter keys, and Kay felt the sigh tunnel through her spine and felt the cool metal keys of the typewriter thrown hot and hard behind her eyes. She went upstairs, not wanting to see her mother's slow ascent, wrapped in her father's brown tweed arms.

Kay could hear him through her bedroom door, talking urgently on the phone, muffling his voice like a Nazi spy; rummaging in the bedroom, dragging the zipper on her mother's ancient overnight bag. She couldn't hear her mother at all.

"All right, we're going. Kay? I'll—we'll be back later. Kay? Please come out of your room and say good-bye."

Kay pulled herself off her bed and stood in her doorway. "'Bye. Have a good time. Have fun."

Laura looked in her direction and right past her. Martin waved his hand widely, as though from a departing plane.

"All right, Kay. Take it easy. I'll call you if I need to. Don't wait up, tomorrow's a school day."

"Yes, I know. Thank you for telling me."

Martin rolled his eyes and opened the door, pulling Laura through it, still gentle even when she just stood there as if she didn't know what doors were for.

He came back the next day, without Laura. He told Kay that her mother needed a complete rest and would be home in a few weeks. He was brisk and oddly cheerful, displaying her mother's upbeat stoicism as though he had stolen it.

For the next two weeks, they lived together as they had when Laura was in the basement. Martin brought home dinner, and Kay cleaned the kitchen. She ran all her father's dark and light clothes together and washed his sweaters in hot water until he stopped making her do the laundry. She met a new girl, Rachel Gevins, and on weekends she slept over at her house and they drank rum and Cokes while the Gevinses were out at the movies. Rachel told Kay that her mother got electrolysis on her stomach. Kay told Rachel that her mother had freaked out and her father had carted her off to a funny farm. Rachel laughed and looked sad and didn't say anything, and Kay knew what it was to trust someone.

When Kay came home from her second weekend at Rachel's, she went down to the basement. "Gripping the wrought-iron banister, Dominique Beauvoir prepared to enter her past . . . " Blake, whom Kay had been surreptitiously feeding tuna fish and boned fried chicken, was gone. The litter box was gone, and so was the ten-pound bag of kitty litter. The table, the chair, the poetry books, the journals, and the cot and pillows were gone. The typewriter was gone. The air carried only faint scents of camphor and cigarettes and cat.

Kay stood in the basement, pushing out deep, uneven breaths. She will never forgive him. Beginning right now, she will never speak to him again. When Kay was little, she would walk from school to her father's office and he would lift her right onto his desk and clear a place for her among the papers so she could swing her legs over the side while she drank cocoa from the mug with the sailboats on it. He introduced her to all the pretty girls who came in and out, and they all smiled at her in a nice way and played with her hair and stood very close to her father. When she was ten, he started locking the office door, and then he said she was old enough to walk straight home by herself. Kay thought he was ashamed of her, and she was ashamed too. She wrote terrible things about him on the wall behind her dresser, but it didn't help.

If her mother does not come back now, when Kay grows up she will hire someone to murder him. Like that girl in New Jersey, she will hire some stupid guy to shoot her father in the head one night while he's reading Thomas Hardy, and she will say she doesn't know anything about it. She cries until she can barely see and locks herself in her bedroom.

When he got home, Martin rattled the doorknob a couple of times, insisting that Kay let him in. He didn't really want her to, and when she didn't, he shrugged and ate most of the fried chicken he had brought home for the two of them. He went to bed, nauseated, hating his life, still surprised by it.

Kay wouldn't leave her room the next morning, and after a few minutes Martin stopped pounding on the door. He had a breakfast meeting, and he said, feeling generous, "It won't kill you to miss a day of school, I guess. Your mother'll be home a little later anyway." He left, relieved that he had spared himself another splenetic fight.

When Kay hears the car grinding out of the driveway, she opens her door and goes back to the basement. She is waiting for a sign, and she wants to believe that she can sit there forever, that she is stonewalling God, not the other way around. The basement is not quite empty, and from her lookout on the stairs Kay can see the scraps that have been left behind. She examines the stubby pencil; nothing special, not even a tooth mark or a broken point. Kay puts it in her pocket and goes over to the corner where the cot had been. On the floor is an empty Dunhills packet, gold foil flowering out of the red box. Kay goes to her room and puts the box in her underwear drawer, tiny tobacco flakes drifting onto her white panties. She puts on her black jeans and an old black sweatshirt, turning it inside out to hide the bright lettering. She would wear a head-band if she had one. Kay hears the car again and stands in the living room, waiting to see just who her father brings home.

She can hear them coming through the kitchen, hears her father grunting as he lugs in the suitcase, hears her mother murmuring thanks. Kay is barely breathing.

Her mother comes into the living room, unsmiling. Someone has dressed her in her khaki skirt and white turtleneck, but the brown belt is missing and her shirttail waves in and out of the waistband.

Kay wants to speak softly, to use her father's basement voice to win her mother back; they will read poetry and eat pizza, and in the end he will shrivel up and blow away, leaving nothing behind but his dorky black shoes. They will be fine then.

"Where's Blake?" is what she says, and her mother's mouth bunches in familiar, ugly ruffles.

"Here we go," says her father, looking at his wife.

"Well? That's not an unreasonable question, is it? I mean, the cat's just gone, you know? You know that, right, Mom? Blake's gone. He had him put to sleep or something."

Kay's mother puts her hand to her forehead, also a familiar gesture, and goes to the bedroom without looking Kay's way. Martin follows her, carrying her suitcase carefully.

In the rich late-morning light, Kay locks her bedroom door and throws the black clothes under her bed. She takes out the smooth red box and unfolds the gold foil, sniffing. Kay lies down and closes her eyes. She falls asleep, the red box clasped beneath her pillow.

Psychoanalysis Changed My Life

For three weeks, four days a week, Marianne told her dreams to Dr. Zurmer. Fat, naked women handed her bouquets of tiger lilies; incomprehensible signs and directories punctuated silent gray corridors; bodiless penises spewed azalea blossoms in great pink and purple arcs. She also talked about her marriage, her divorce, and her parents. Behind her, Dr. Zurmer nodded and took notes and occasionally slipped her knotted, elderly feet out of elegant black velvet flats, wiggling her toes until she could feel her blood begin to move. Marianne could hear her even and attentive breathing, could hear the occasional light scratch of her cigarlike fountain pen.

At the end of another long dream, in which Marianne's father frantically attempted to reach Marianne through steadily drifting petals, Dr. Zurmer put down her pen.

"Why don't you sit up, Dr. Loewe?"

Marianne didn't move, still thinking of the soft drifts and the few white petals that had clung to her father's beard as he struggled toward her. Dr. Zurmer thought she had shocked her patient into immobility.

"After all, there are two of us in the room. Why should we pretend that only one of us is real, that only one of us is present?"

Marianne sat up.

"All these white flower dreams," Dr. Zurmer said, "what are they about?"

"I'm sure they're about my mother. I don't know if you remember, my mother's name was Lily. And she was like a white flower, thin, pale, graceful. Just wafting around, not a solid person at all. Just a little bit of everything, you know, real estate, house painting, for a while she read tea leaves in some fake Gypsy restaurant. I mean, now she's a businesswoman, but then ... My father was the stable one, but she drove him away."

Dr. Zurmer said, "He was stable, but he disappeared. You say she was 'wafting around,' but she never left you. And she always made a living, yes?"

"He didn't disappear. My mother was having an affair, one of many, I'm sure, she was such a fucking belle of the ball, and he couldn't stand it and he left." Marianne was glad that she could say "fucking."

"It's understandable that he would choose to end the marriage. Not everyone would, but it's understandable. But why did he stop seeing you?"

"He didn't really have much choice. She got custody somehow, and then he moved to California for his work. I went to California once, for about a week, but then, I don't know, he remarried, and then he died in a car accident." Marianne started to cry and wished she were back on the couch, invisible.

"How old were you when you went to California?"

"Nine."

"How did you get there?"

"My mother took me by plane."

"Your mother took you by plane to California so you could visit your father?"

"Sometimes she was overprotective. I remember he said that when I was old enough to take the plane by myself I could come out there. I thought nine was old enough, but my mother took me."

"Of course. Why would you send a nine-year-old three thousand miles away by herself, unless it was an emergency?"

"Lots of people do."

"Lots of people behave selfishly and irresponsibly. It doesn't seem that your father thought nine was really old enough either. He, however, was willing to wait another year or two before you saw each other."

"It wasn't like that."

"I think it was. You are almost forty now. I am almost eighty-five. We are not going to have time for a long analysis, Dr. Loewe, which is just as well. I will tell you what I see, when I see something, but you have to be willing to look. Your mother knew how important your father was to you, and even though your father had left her, she was willing to take the time and money to make sure that you saw him, even in the face of his indifference. You must think about why you need your father to be the hero of this story. Tomorrow, yes?"

Marianne went home, less happy than she had been the first time they met. Three weeks ago, walking into that gray-carpeted waiting room, with its two black-and-white Sierra Club photographs and the dusty mahogany coffee table offering only last week's *Paris-Match* and last year's *New Yorkers*, Marianne knew that she was in sure and authentic hands. Despite an unexpected penchant for bright, bulky sweaters, made charming and European by carefully embroidered flowers on the pockets, Dr. Zurmer was just what Marianne had hoped for.

On Tuesday, Dr. Zurmer interrupted Marianne's memory of her grandfather shaving with an old-fashioned straight razor to tell her that beige was not her color.

"Beige is for redheads, for certain blondes. Not for you. My hair was the same color fifty years ago. *Chatin.* Ahh, chestnut. A lovely color, even with the gray. You would look very nice in green, all different greens, like spring leaves. Maybe a ring or a bracelet, as well, to call attention to your pretty hands."

Marianne looked at Dr. Zurmer, and Dr. Zurmer smiled back.

"We must stop for today. Tomorrow, Dr. Loewe."

Marianne went home and fed her cat, and as she put on her navy bathrobe and her backless slippers, she watched herself in the mirror.

During the next week's sessions, Dr. Zurmer gave Marianne the name of a good masseuse, an expert hair colorist, and a store that specialized in narrow-width Swiss shoes, which turned out to be perfect for Marianne's feet and sensibilities. At the end of Thursday's session, Dr. Zurmer suggested that Marianne focus less on the past and more on the present.

"Your mother invites you to her beach house every weekend, Dr. Loewe. Why not go? I don't think she wants to devour you or humiliate you. I think she wants to show off her brilliant daughter to her friends and she wants you to appreciate the life she's made for herself—beach house and catering business and so on. This is no small potatoes for a woman of her background, for the delicate flower you say she is. Life is short, Dr. Loewe. Go visit your mother and see what is really there. At the very worst, you will have escaped this dreadful heat and you will return to tell me that my notions are all wet."

Charmed by Dr. Zurmer's archaic Americanisms and the vision of herself and her mother walking on the beach at sunset, their identical short, strong legs and narrow feet skimming through the sand, Marianne rose to leave, not waiting for Dr. Zurmer's dismissal.

Dr. Zurmer began to rise and could not. Her head fell forward, and her half-moon glasses, which made her look so severe and so kind, landed on the floor.

Marianne crouched beside Dr. Zurmer's chair and put just her fingertips on Dr. Zurmer's shoulder. Dr. Zurmer did not lift her head.

"Please take me home. I am not well."

"Should I call your doctor? Or an ambulance? They can bring you to the hospital."

"I am not going to a hospital. Please take me home." Dr. Zurmer raised her head, and without her glasses she looked extremely vulnerable and reptilian, an ancient turtle, arrogant in its longevity, resigned to its fate.

Terrified, Marianne drove Dr. Zurmer home, regretting the Kleenex and Heath Bar wrappers in the backseat, where Dr. Zurmer lay, pain dampening and distorting the matte, powdery surface of her fine old skin. When they approached a small Spanish-style house with ivy reaching up to the red tile roof and slightly weedy marigolds lining the front walk, Dr. Zurmer indicated that Marianne should pull into the driveway. Marianne could not imagine carrying Dr. Zurmer up the walk, although she was probably capable of lifting her, but she didn't think Dr. Zurmer could make the hundred yards on her own.

"Is someone home? I can go let them know that you're here, and they can give us a hand."

Dr. Zurmer nodded twice, and her head sagged back against the seat.

A thin old man, shorter than Marianne and leaning hard on a rubber-tipped cane, opened the door. Marianne explained what had happened, even mentioning that she was Dr. Zurmer's patient, which was a weird and embarrassing thing to have to say to the man who was obviously her analyst's husband. He nodded and followed Marianne out to the car. It was clear to Marianne that this little old man was in no position to carry his wife to the house, and that she, Marianne, would have to stick around for a few more minutes and take Dr. Zurmer in, probably to her bedroom, perhaps to her bathroom, which was not a pleasant thought.

"Otto," was all Dr. Zurmer said.

They spoke softly in Russian, and Marianne gently pulled Dr. Zurmer from the backseat, handing her briefcase to the husband, half carrying, half dragging Dr. Zurmer up the walk under his critical, anxious eye. Dr. Zurmer's husband seemed not to speak English, or not to speak to people other than his wife.

Marianne was so focused on not dropping Dr. Zurmer and following Mr. or Dr. Zurmer's hand signals that she barely saw her analyst's house, although she had wondered about it, with occasional, pleasurable intensity, in the last three weeks. Dr. Zurmer slipped out of Marianne's arms onto a large bed covered with a white lace spread and said thank you and goodbye. Marianne, who had not wanted to come and had not wanted to stay, felt that this was a little abrupt, even ungracious, but she was polite and said it was no trouble and that she would find her own way out so that they would not be disturbed. The old man had lain down next to his wife and was wiping her damp face with his handkerchief.

Marianne walked down the narrow, turning staircase, noticing the scratched brass rods that anchored the faded green carpeting, and looking into the faces in the framed photographs that dotted the wall beside her like dark windows. Two skinny boys in baggy dark trunks are building a huge, turreted sand castle trimmed with seashells, twigs, and the remains of horseshoe crabs, surrounded by a moat that reaches up to the knees of a younger, taller Otto Zurmer. In another, the two skinny boys are now skinny teenagers sitting on a stone wall, back to back like bookends, in matching sunglasses, matching bare chests, and matching fearless and immortal grins.

Marianne was conscious of lingering, of trespassing, in fact, and she only took one quick look at the photograph that interested her the most. Dr. Zurmer, whose first name, Anya, Marianne had read on the brass plaque of her office door, is sitting in a velvet armchair, legs stretched sideways and crossed at the slender white silk ankles. She cannot be more than twenty, and she looks pampered, with her lace-trimmed dress and carefully curled hair, and she looks beautiful; she peers uncertainly at the viewer, eager and afraid.

Marianne spent the next week working harder on the book she was trying to write, staking the tomato plants in her small yard, and getting her hair colored. It came out eye-catching and rich, the color of fine luggage, the color of expensive brandy, the kind drunk only by handsome old men sitting in wing armchairs by their early-evening fires. Marianne was tempted to wear a scarf until the color faded, but she could not bear to cover it up, and at night she fanned it out on her pillow and admired what she could see of the fine, gleaming strands.

She waited to hear from Dr. Zurmer and decided that if she didn't get word from her by Friday, she would leave a message with the answering service. On Friday, Dr. Zurmer called. She told Marianne that she was not yet well enough to return to the office but could see her for a session at home. She did not ask Marianne how she felt about meeting with her therapist, in her therapist's home, with little Dr./Mr. Zurmer running in and out, she simply inquired whether Monday at nine would suit her. That was their usual time, and Marianne said yes and hung up the phone quickly so as not to tire Dr. Zurmer, who sounded terrible.

Dr. Zurmer's husband let Marianne in silently, but when she was fully through the door he took her hand in both of his and thanked her, in perfectly good English.

"Please call me Otto," he said. His smile was very kind, and Marianne said her name and was pleased with them both.

Dr. Zurmer sat in bed, propped up by dozens of large and small Battenberg lace pillows, her silver hair brushed, neat and sleek as mink. She wore a remarkably businesslike grey satin bed jacket. Marianne couldn't tell if Dr. Zurmer's face was slightly longer and looser than before or if she had forgotten, in a week, exactly what Dr. Zurmer looked like.

"I feel much better today. A very tiny stroke, my doctor said. And no harm done, apparently. Thank you, Dr. Loewe. So, I will lie down during our sessions and you will sit up."

Marianne began by telling Dr. Zurmer her latest flower dream but wrapped it up quickly in order to talk about the photograph of Dr. Zurmer, not mentioning the boys; and she sat back in the little brocade chair, looking at the ceiling, in order to talk about the dislocating, fascinating oddness of being in Dr. Zurmer's house. Dr. Zurmer smiled, shaking her head sympathetically, and fell asleep. Marianne sat quietly, only a little insulted, and watched Dr. Zurmer breathe. At her elbow was a mahogany dresser laid over with embroidered, crocheted runners, four small photographs in silver frames and three perfume bottles of striped Murano glass sitting on top. The little gold-tipped bottles were almost empty. One photograph, as Marianne expected, shows the two young men from the stone wall and the beach, a good bit older, both in suits. They are clearly at a wedding, with linen-covered tables and gladioli behind them, although there is no bride in sight. Another shows Dr. Zurmer and Otto, their arms around each other, in front of the lighthouse at Gay Head, and the picture is not unlike one of Marianne and her ex-husband, at that same spot, during the brief, good time of their marriage. The other two photographs are of a dark-skinned woman in a bathrobe, holding what must be a baby wrapped in a blue and white blanket, and finally, a very little boy with black curls, jug ears, and the same slightly slant, long-lashed eyes as the woman.

As Marianne reached the front door, Otto clumped toward her.

"Tea?" he said, waving his cane toward the back of the house.

Marianne said no and went home to look up the phone numbers of other psychoanalysts.

On Thursday, Otto called. "Please come today," he said. "She wants to see you."

Marianne had already set up a consultation with another analyst, a middle-aged man with a good reputation and an office overlooking the river, but she went.

Dr. Zurmer was sitting up again, her bed jacket open over a flannel nightgown and her hair tufted in downy silver puffs.

She stretched out her hand for Marianne's and held onto it as Marianne sat down, much closer than planned.

"It seems that I am not well enough to be your analyst after all. But I don't think we should let that stop us from enjoying each other's company, do you? You come and visit, and we'll have tea."

Marianne could not imagine why Dr. Zurmer wanted her to visit.

"Why not? You're smart, a very kind person, you have a wonderful imagination and sense of humor—I see that in your dreams—why shouldn't I want you to visit me? Otto will bring us tea. Sit."

Over pale green tea swarming with brown bits of leaf, Marianne and Dr. Zurmer smiled at each other.

"I was very interested in the photographs on your dresser," Marianne said.

"What about them interests you?"

"This is just a visit, remember? Tea and conversation."

Dr. Zurmer pretended to slap her own wrist and smiled broadly at Marianne, her cheeks folding up like silk ruching.

"Touché," she said. "Bring the photos over here, please. And there's an album in the magazine rack there.

"Oh, look at this, little Alexei. Everyone has these bathtub photographs tucked away. And this is Alexei in Cub Scouts, I think that lasted for six months. He loved the uniform, but he was not, not Scout material. And this is him with his brother, Robert. You saw some of these on the wall, I think. At Martha's Vineyard. We used to stay at a little farmhouse, two bedrooms and a tiny kitchen. Friends of Otto's lent it to us every summer. Otto designed their house, the big house in the background here, and their house, I forget, in the suburbs of Boston. We were the house pets, but it was wonderful for the children. This is Robert's college graduation. I can't remember what all the armbands represent, he protested everything. Unfortunately for him, we were liberals, so it was difficult to disturb us. He did become a banker, there was that. And here is Alexei graduating, no armbands, just the hair. But it was such beautiful hair, I wanted him to keep it long, I thought he looked like Apollo. And here are the wedding pictures, Alexei and his wife, Naria. Lebanese. They met in graduate school. And this is my only grandson, Lee. As beautiful as the day. As good as he is beautiful. Very bright child. Alexei is a wonderful father, father and mother both. This big one is Lee last year, on his fourth birthday. That's his favorite bear, I don't remember now, the train station name."

"Paddington. He's lovely. Lee is just lovely."

"Naria left them almost two years ago. She has a narcissistic personality disorder. She simply could not mother. People cannot do what they are not equipped to do. So, she's gone, back to Lebanon. Also, very self-destructive, to return to a place like Lebanon, divorced, a mother, clearly not a virgin. She will care for her father, in his home, for the rest of her life. Who can say? Perhaps that was her wish."

Dr. Zurmer said "narcissistic personality disorder" the way you'd say "terminal cancer," and Marianne nodded, understanding that Naria was gone from this earth.

"And this is a picture Alexei took of me and Otto two years ago. Those two lovers, the gods made them into trees, or bushes? Philomena? So that they might never part. We look like that, yes? Already beginning to merge with the earth."

Dr. Zurmer lay back, and the album slid between them.

"I cannot really speak of loving him anymore. Does one love the brain, or the heart? Does one appreciate one's blood? We have kept each other from the worst loneliness, and we listen to each other. We don't say anything very interesting anymore, we talk of Lee, of Alexei, we remember Robert . . . "

Marianne waited for the terrible story.

"He died in a car accident, right after the wedding. I am still grieving and I am still angry. He was drinking too much, that was something he did. Alexei, never. My bad Russian genes. He left nothing behind, an apartment full of junk, a job he disliked, debts. I thought perhaps a pregnant girlfriend would emerge, but that didn't happen. I would have made it so, if I could have. I have to rest, my dear."

Dr. Zurmer sank back into her pillows and asked Marianne to go into the bottom drawer of the mahogany dresser. Marianne brought her the only thing in it, a bolt of green satin, thick and cool, rippling in her hands like something alive. Dr. Zurmer tied it around her waist, turning Marianne's white shirt and khaki slacks into something dashing, exotic, and slightly, delightfully androgynous.

"Just so. When you leave, please say good-bye to Otto. He likes you so much. 'Such a luffly girl,'" she said, mimicking Otto's accent, which was, if anything, less noticeable, less guttural, than her own. "If he's not in the kitchen, just wait a minute. He's probably getting the newspaper, going for his constitutional. Be well, Marianne. Come again soon."

The man sitting at the kitchen table was so clearly the slightly bigger boy from the photographs, the bearded groom, that Marianne smiled at him familiarly, filled with tenderness and receptivity, as though her pores were steaming open. He stared back at her and then, with great, courtly gestures, folded the newspaper and slid it behind the toaster.

"You must be Marianne."

"Yes. I just wanted to say good-bye to your father, I'm on my way home," she said.

"That will please him. I'm Alex Zurmer. I don't know where Pop is." He looked at her again, at her deep brown eyes and long neck, his own sweet baby giraffe, and watched her blunt, bony fingers playing with the fringe of the glimmering green sash. Alex shrugged, lifting his palms heavenward, as awestruck and grateful as Noah, knowing that he had been selected for survival and the arrival of doves. He watched Marianne's restless, slightly bitten fingers twisting in and out of the thick tasseled ends, and he could feel them touching his face, lifting his hair.

"Let's have tea while we wait. Marianne," he said, and he rose to pull out her chair, and she very deliberately laid her hand next to his on the back of the chair.

"Let's," said Marianne. "Let's put out a few cookies too. If you use loose tea, I'll read the leaves."

Acknowledgments

Many thanks to the talented editors at Burlingame Books, with whom I first worked: Kathy Banks, for her sharp editorial eye and strong early encouragement, and Ed Burlingame, for his tremendous faith and efforts. I can only indicate how grateful I am to Joy Johannessen of Aaron Asher Books, an editorial archangel; she is demanding and generous, giving and expecting only the best.

I thank my agent, Phyllis Wender, who has led me through unknown and peculiar territory kindly, firmly, intelligently, and with class and common sense.

I am grateful to the Sydelle J. Bloom Foundation for Daughters Who Write for its enthusiastic support.

My two dearest and earliest reader-friends, Kay Ariel and Malcolm Keith, provided thoughtful responses, careful criticism, and loving appreciation, the last of which I return, by the truckload.

I also thank my three children, my jewels, Alexander, Caitlin, and Sarah, who have all contributed inestimably to my writing and to my life.

Finally, this collection would be less than it is if not for the extraordinary contributions of Donald Moon, who understands computers, numbers, deadlines, anxiety, fiction, and me.